available at

BARNES
&NOBLE

Editor's Picks

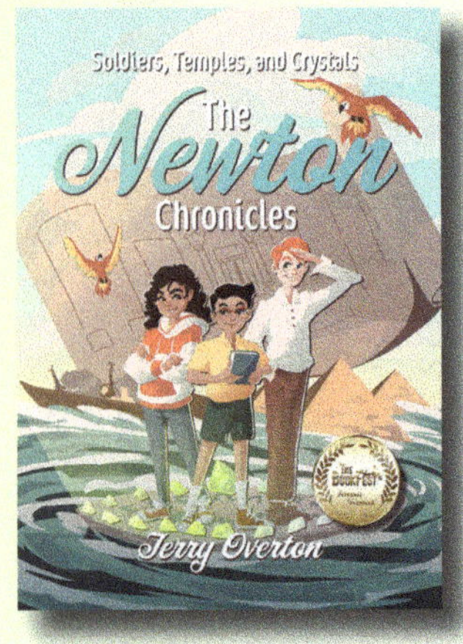

Soldiers, Temples, and Crystals

TERRY OVERTON

"An enthralling journey through time, blending history, mystery, and adventure with captivating characters and a richly woven narrative tapestry."

Paperback: £12.99

https://amzn.to/3Tq3Jso

The Good, the Bad, and the Aunties

JESSE SUTANTO

"Jesse Sutanto's book is a hilarious, heartwarming adventure filled with unforgettable characters and delightful twists."

Kindle: £8.61

https://amzn.to/4elThKm

Ellie The Crop Duster Saves The Farm

REBECCA VICTOR

"Rebecca Victor's charming tale of Ellie inspires with its delightful adventure, heartwarming themes, and vibrant storytelling."

Paperback: £16.14

https://amzn.to/3MHxyRo

Kicking Out The Bucket List

GLENDA MITCHELL

"A transformative journey, inspiring readers to live with purpose and embrace life's adventures with intention.

*"Paperback £15.49

https://amzn.to/4enOdVN

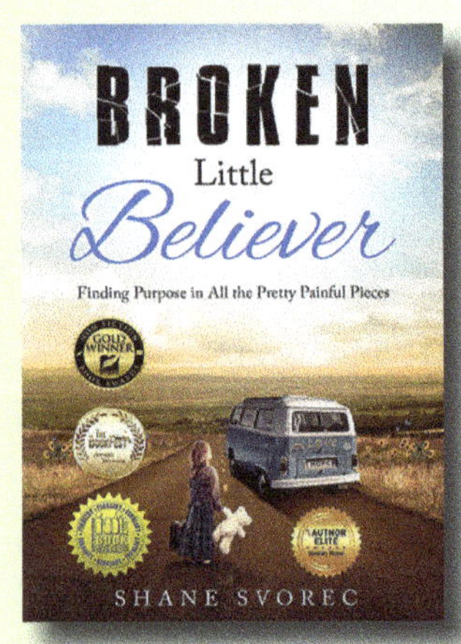

Broken Little Believer

SHANE SVOREC

"A heartfelt journey of resilience and hope, inspiring readers to find purpose amidst life's challenges."

Hardcove: £12.43

https://amzn.to/4cPQTv7

A Love to Die For

JOSEPH SEECHACK

"A captivating exploration of love and mortality, offering profound insights and emotional depth in every chapter."

Paperback: £13.95

https://amzn.to/3XHpVAF

Empowered Woman

ADEBOLA AJAO

"A transformative guide empowering women to unlock their potential, offering practical wisdom and inspiring principles."

Paperback: £17.88

https://amzn.to/3XJ4krD

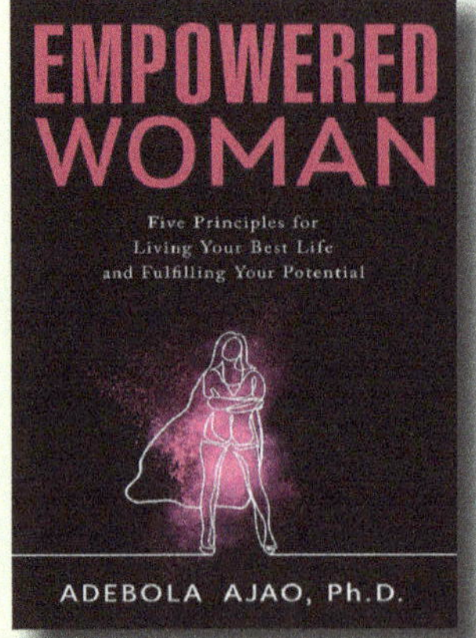

Utopia Falling

R.C. VIELEE

"Utopia Falling" captivates with its thrilling plot, rich world-building, and unforgettable characters. A must-read adventure!"

paperback: £19.99

https://amzn.to/4d5fmfi

Your Gateway to Endless Stories

Escaping My Demons

JOSEPH FAGARAZZI

"Escaping My Demons is a hard-hitting, riveting, emotional memoir by Joseph Fagarazzi! The book focuses on the turbulent and tense relationships between Joseph and his parents, particularly his selfish, abusive, and exploitative father. "

– Steven Setil

Kindle: £7.95

https://amzn.to/3xZ4Mbg

Consoling Angel

DENISE ALICEA

"Consoling Angel beautifully weaves time travel, romance, and healing into an unforgettable, heartwarming narrative."

Kindle: £0.99

https://amzn.to/4gpiIMO

Being Alice

MICHELE OLSON

"Enchanting tales beautifully capture Mackinac's charm, weaving nostalgia and wonder into every page. A delightful read!"

Paperback: £12.99

https://amzn.to/3z8XKkRV

Her Best Defense

CORDELL PARVIN

"Her Best Defense captivates with its thrilling plot, strong characters, and masterful storytelling."

Hardcove: £15.54

https://amzn.to/3MMz6JS

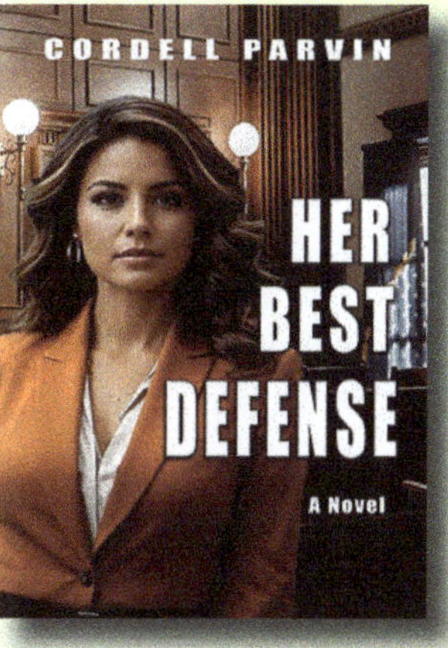

The Secret History

R. H. EMMERS

"A gripping, hard-boiled thriller weaving crime, politics, and loyalty into a masterful tale of vengeance."

Paperback: £7.19

https://amzn.to/4gqnppB

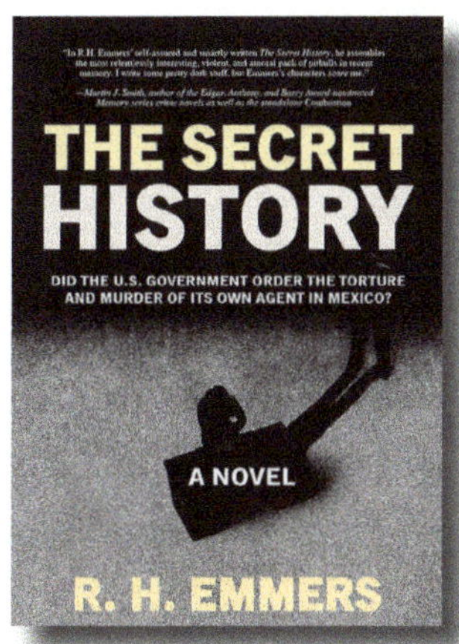

Grace Ungiven

JEFF KELLAND

"Grace Ungiven masterfully blends truth and fiction, delivering a powerful, compassionate narrative on justice and redemption."

Hardcover: £16.67

https://amzn.to/3XIRsl5

Murder On His Mind

ANNE PENN

"This gripping book masterfully unravels the chilling tale of the Golden State Killer's heinous crimes."

Paperback: £14.24

https://amzn.to/4d19zas

Loudening Silence

WENDY ZUCCARELLO

"Loudening Silence captivates with its profound storytelling, exploring deep emotions and human resilience in remarkable ways."

Paperback: £10.73

https://amzn.to/3TqObo4

IN THIS ISSUE

Behind the Books. A Closer Look
In-depth Interviews with Celebrated Authors

12
ON THE COVER

Unveiling the Literary Brilliance of
MICHELLE M. PILLOW
Inviting Readers Into Her Enchanting Worlds
Michelle M. Pillow, New York Times and USA Today bestselling author, discusses her diverse genres, creative process, and global impact, inviting readers into her enchanting worlds.

SCAN TO READ ONLINE

EDITOR'S LETTER

Dear Readers,
It is with great excitement and pride that we present to you the 47th issue of Reader's House Magazine. This edition is a celebration of storytelling in its most enchanting forms, and we are thrilled to feature an exclusive interview with the illustrious Michelle M. Pillow, a New York Times and USA TODAY bestselling author whose works have captivated the hearts and imaginations of millions.

Michelle M. Pillow is a master of her craft, weaving tales that transport readers to worlds where romance, mystery, and adventure intertwine seamlessly. Her ability to create rich, immersive worlds and vibrant characters is unparalleled, and her stories serve as portals to the imagination. In our exclusive interview, Pillow shares insights into her creative process, the inspiration behind her beloved series, and her dedication to crafting unforgettable narratives. Her humility and passion for storytelling shine through, offering sage advice for aspiring writers and a glimpse into the mind of a literary luminary.

In addition to our feature on Michelle M. Pillow, this issue is brimming with interviews from a diverse array of award-winning authors, each bringing their unique voice and perspective to the literary landscape. We are honoured to include conversations with Linda O. Johnston, Chris Bohjalian, Shane Svorec, S.M. Stevens, Jack Erickson, Cristina Leport, P.C. James, Jeff Kelland, Sandy Rosenthal, Lucinda Brant, Angel Giacomo, Joseph Fagarazzi, Terry Lister, Sarah Albee, Len Handeland, Thomas J. Yeggy, Julie Anderson, and Terrence A. Reese. These exceptional authors share their journeys, inspirations, and the stories that have shaped their careers.

At Reader's House, we believe in the transformative power of literature. Books have the ability to entertain, educate, and provide solace during challenging times. They open doors to new worlds and perspectives, allowing us to explore the depths of human experience. In this issue, we invite you to embark on a literary journey that promises to inspire, challenge, and delight.

As you turn the pages of this issue, we hope you find stories that resonate with you, characters that linger in your thoughts, and worlds that ignite your imagination. We are grateful for your continued support and enthusiasm for the written word, and we look forward to sharing many more literary adventures with you.

Happy reading!

A, Harlowe

Editor's Desk

PUBLISHER
Reader's House
A Subsidiary of Newyox Media
https://newyox.media

200 Suite
134-146 Curtain Road
EC2A 3AR London
t: +44 79 3847 8420

editor@readershouse.co.uk
readershouse.co.uk

EDITORIAL
A. Harlowe
editor@readershouse.co.uk
Dan Peters
dan.peters@readershouse.co.uk
Ben Alan
ben.alan@readershouse.co.uk

CONTRIBUTORS
Claudine D. Reyes
Acacia Baldie
Andrea Piacquadio
Adrian T. Cheng
Donna Schim
Jon Allo
Tim Halloran
Oleg Magni
Amir SeilSepour
Bill Youngblood
Jetty Stutzman
Jimmy Choo
Peter Filinovich
Rrodnae Productions

Reader's House

readershouse.co.uk

We assume no responsibility for unsolicited manuscripts or art materials provided from our contributors.

Linda O. Johnston, celebrated author of over 60 novels, shares her journey and inspirations with Reader's House Magazine

From Legal Briefs to Romantic Thrills

LINDA O. JOHNSTON

EXPLORING THE HEARTFELT NARRATIVES AND MYSTERIES

AS TOLD TO CHIARA ROCCIA

Linda O. Johnston is a name synonymous with romance and mystery, her storytelling blending heartfelt relationships with gripping suspense. From her earliest days, Linda knew she was destined to write, weaving narratives even as a child that hinted at the prolific career to come. With an impressive portfolio of over 60 novels spanning various subgenres, she has captivated readers with tales of love, intrigue, and, notably, a deep affection for animals.

Linda's writing journey began early, with childhood stories that showcased her burgeoning talent and imagination. Despite a temporary hiatus during law school, her passion for storytelling soon resurfaced. Her legal background added a unique layer to her writing, enriching her narratives with authenticity and detail. She began with short stories, one of which won the Robert L. Fish Memorial Award, before transitioning to full-length novels. Her debut novel, the time-travel romance "A Glimpse of Forever," marked the beginning of a diverse and successful career.

A trained lawyer turned full-time author; Linda's journey is as dynamic as her plots. Her commitment to crafting intricate stories that often highlight the bond between humans and animals is evident in beloved series like the Pet Rescue Mysteries and Kendra Ballantyne, Pet-Sitter Mysteries. Her work reflects a genuine passion for animal rights, bringing a unique depth to her characters and settings.

"CSI Colton and the Witness" is an engaging addition to the Coltons of New York series. Linda O. Johnston masterfully blends romance and suspense, creating a thrilling narrative that keeps readers on the edge of their seats. The characters are well-developed, with CSI Colton standing out as a compelling protagonist whose dedication to justice is both admirable and relatable. The plot is intricately woven, with enough twists and turns to keep the reader guessing until the very end. Fans of romantic suspense will find this book hard to put down. Highly recommended for those who enjoy a good mix of mystery and romance.

In our interview, Linda delves into her inspiration for the Shelter of Secrets series, a fascinating blend of animal rescue and human drama, as well as her Alaska Untamed Mystery series, born from her own adventures in the Alaskan wilderness. She shares how her love for cruises and the natural world of Alaska sparked the creation of Stacie Calder, a naturalist and sleuth navigating the rugged beauty of the last frontier. Linda's attention to detail and commitment to authenticity

> Linda O. Johnston masterfully blends romance, suspense, and animal advocacy, captivating readers with her heartfelt and thrilling storytelling.

shine through as she discusses her research methods and the joys of setting a series in such a unique location.

Linda also offers a glimpse into the challenges and rewards of contributing to long-running series like the Colton series, where multiple authors collaborate to expand a vast fictional family. Her ability to craft engaging, standalone stories within this framework speaks to her versatility and skill as a writer.

A dedicated member of several writers' organizations, including the Romance Writers of America and Sisters in Crime, Linda emphasizes the importance of community and continuous learning in a writer's journey. She offers valuable advice to aspiring writers on embracing their passions across multiple genres, encouraging them to find their voice and persist through the editing process.

Join us as Linda O. Johnston takes us behind the scenes of her creative process, her love for animals, and the heart-pounding excitement of romantic suspense. Her journey from writing short stories to becoming an award-winning author is as compelling as the stories she tells.

Your latest book, "Canine Protection," is the fourth in the Shelter of Secrets series. Can you tell us more about what inspired this series and its unique premise of a shelter that protects both animals and people?

I am an absolute dog lover and very much believe in caring for and adopting rescue animals—although I'm a bit of a hypocrite about it since my dogs for many years have been Cavalier King Charles Spaniels and I have adopted them from reputable breeders because of the breed's health issues. But I love writing about shelters, and the idea of one that also took in people in trouble and created new identities for them really inspired me to start writing the Shelter of Secrets series for Harlequin Romantic Suspense. The series is winding down though, and there will only be one more after "Canine Protection," titled "Canine Refuge" next year, because with all that has occurred at and around the fictional shelter in the existing books the place might not be as much of a secret if it continued.

Your Alaska Untamed Mystery series introduces readers to Stacie Calder, a naturalist in Alaska. What inspired you to set this series in such a unique location, and how do you conduct research for it?

I love to go on cruises with my husband, and our most recent cruise was to Alaska a few years ago—probably my fifth Alaskan cruise. When we spent time in Juneau there we had the opportunity to go on a river tour that was given by local naturalists who pointed out a lot of the wildlife in the area—and that inspired me to write about it. I even started asking questions and doing research on that tour boat. Stacie Calder was the result, an educated naturalist who also gives tours in Alaska—and solves crimes, sometimes after dead bodies are spotted in the water off the tour boats! And of course Stacie brings her own beloved husky Sasha with her each day.

What are some of the challenges you face when continuing long-running series like the Colton series?

The Colton series is definitely fun to write for! The books are actually works for hire by Harlequin Romantic Suspense because each year a new part of the vast fictional Colton family is featured, and the contents of the individual stories are determined by Harlequin but written by various authors in their lineup. My most significant challenge is to come up with an enjoyable rendering of the story that I'm designated to write.

Many of your books, including the Pet Rescue Mysteries and Kendra Ballantyne, Pet-Sitter Mysteries, feature strong animal themes. What draws you to write about animals and their relationships with humans?

As I mentioned, I'm a total dog nut, and I really enjoy writing about them. I'm also an advocate for animal rights in general and love reading and hearing about –and viewing—wildlife as well. Writing about animals makes me happy, and I hope it make my readers happy too.

What do you enjoy most about writing romantic suspense?

I enjoy coming up with characters who are attracted to one another but also get into some challenging situations where they have to sometimes save their own lives and each other's, while their attraction continues to build into something that will affect their entire lives.

What advice would you give to aspiring writers who are interested in writing across multiple genres and incorporating their personal passions, like animals, into their work?

Just do it! Determine what you want to write and figure out the best genre or genres for it. And then start writing, and continue till your stories are complete, then spend significant time editing them. It helps to join writers' organizations in your favourite genres and learn from the other members, as well as joining critique groups.

Chris Bohjalian discusses his inspirations, research, and character development, reflecting on his diverse novels, screen adaptations, and the personal significance of his work on the Armenian Genocide.

Chris Bohjalian, the acclaimed author of 24 novels, including bestsellers like Midwives and The Flight Attendant.

Master Storyteller of Our Time

CHRIS BOHJALIAN

EXPLORING THE INSPIRATIONS BEHIND 24 BESTSELLING NOVELS

BY DAN PETERS

Chris Bohjalian is a literary force whose prolific career has spanned 24 books, including the acclaimed titles Midwives, The Flight Attendant, and the eagerly anticipated The Jackal's Mistress. His works have not only captivated readers worldwide, being translated into over 35 languages, but have also found their way to the screen, becoming three movies and a TV series. Beyond his novels, Bohjalian is also a playwright, showcasing his versatility and depth as a storyteller. Residing in Vermont with his wife, Victoria Blewer, Bohjalian continues to explore diverse themes and historical periods with a fervor that keeps him at his desk at the crack of dawn.

In this exclusive interview with Reader's House Magazine, Bohjalian delves into the inspirations behind his varied works, from the historical intricacies of the 17th century in Hour of the Witch to the deeply personal narrative of The Sandcastle Girls, which addresses the Armenian Genocide. He shares insights into his meticulous research process, character development techniques, and the emotional resonance he strives to achieve in his novels. Bohjalian also reflects on the experience of seeing his work adapted for the screen, particularly the success of The Flight Attendant, and offers a glimpse into his latest novel, The Princess of Las Vegas. Join us as we explore the mind of one of today's most compelling authors.

With a prolific career spanning 24 books and adaptations into movies and TV series, what inspires you to keep writing, and how do you decide on the themes or stories you want to explore in your novels?

My goal is never to write the same book twice. I write about anything that interests me -- and interests me with the sort of fervor that will propel me to my desk at six in the morning. If I'm not willing to be at my desk at the crack of dawn, that's an indication that whatever I'm doing isn't working, and it's time to abort mission and explore something new.

Chris Bohjalian is a literary genius whose compelling narratives and meticulous research captivate readers and critics alike.

Hour of the Witch delves into the historical context of the 17th century and the harrowing experiences of a young Puritan woman. What drew you to this period, and what kind of research did you undertake to authentically portray the challenges and societal norms of that time?

I've been fascinated by Puritan theology since I studied it in college. Imagine living in a world where Satan is as real as your neighbor, and you spend much of your life wondering if you're saved or damned, and always looking for signs. The research wasn't hard because the Puritans were avid diarists and kept astonishing court records. And the fact that Puritan women divorced their husbands over adultery, cruelty, polygamy, desertion, and impotence was literary gold. Finally, how can you not love material that allows you to name a fierce and wonderful woman Peregrine?

Your novel The Sandcastle Girls addresses the Armenian Genocide, a deeply emotional and historical topic. How did you approach writing about such a sensitive subject, and what impact do you hope the book has on readers' understanding of this historical event?

I know the impact of the book: it educated countless readers around the world to the horrors of the Armenian Genocide, the Otto-man Empire's systematic annihilation of 1.5 million Armenians, 300 thousand Assyrians, and countless Greeks. It was an international bestseller published in easily 20 languages. Two of my grandparents survived the Armenian Genocide and eventually emigrated to the United States, so this is a deeply personal novel for me, and its success mattered to me as much as any book I have written.

The Flight Attendant was a major hit both as a novel and a TV series. Can you share your thoughts on seeing your work adapted for the screen and how involved you were in the adaptation process?

I loved the series. I thought Kaley Cuoco was brilliant as my damaged flight attendant. My involvement principally involved trying to stay out of everyone's way the few times I was on the set, and devouring blueberries and bagels at craft services.

Many of your novels, like The Sleepwalker and The Red Lotus, feature complex characters dealing with extraordinary situations. How do you develop your characters, and what techniques do you use to ensure they resonate with readers on an emotional level?

I do my homework. For The Night Strangers, for instance, which begins with a plane crashing into Lake Champlain near Burlington, Vermont, I spent a full day in the "dunk tank" with naval aviators learning how to exit a plane that has crashed in water and is sinking fast. That sort of research is critical to character development. Also? I ask experts on the subject – sleepwalking, bioweapons, working in an E.R. – questions that likely are none of my business.

Your latest novel, The Lioness, takes readers on a thrilling journey to the Serengeti in the 1960s. What inspired you to set the story in this unique location and time period, and what themes do you explore through the experiences of your characters in this novel?

First of all, that's not my most recent novel. My most recent novel is The Princess of Las Vegas, a tale of a Princess Diana tribute performer at a shabby, off the strip casino, and her estranged sister. Imagine the TV series, "Hacks" meets "The Crown."

As for The Lioness, I wanted to explore a lot of things: Hollywood's golden age, the devastating legacy of colonialism, and how ordinary people behave when – and I mean this literally and metaphorically – the lions are circling. Yes, it's a thriller, but I hope it also takes a deep dive into what makes us heroes or cowards.

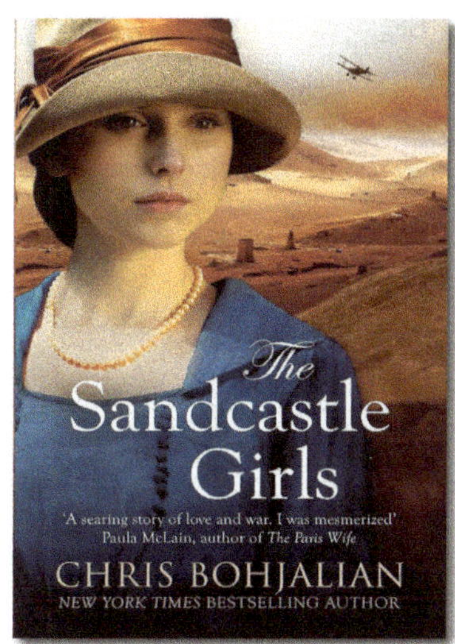

The Sandcastle Girls by Chris Bohjalian is a masterful and haunting novel that intertwines a poignant love story with the harrowing events of the Armenian Genocide. Bohjalian's narrative prowess shines as he transports readers to 1915 Aleppo, where Elizabeth Endicott, a young American woman, confronts unimaginable atrocities with courage and compassion. Her bond with Armen, an Armenian engineer shattered by loss, is both heart-wrenching and inspiring, capturing the resilience of the human spirit amidst the darkest of times.

In the present day, Laura Petrosian's quest to uncover her family's hidden past adds a compelling layer to the story, bridging generations and shedding light on a nation's suffering. Bohjalian's meticulous research and evocative prose bring history to life, making the reader feel every emotion and struggle faced by the characters.

This novel is not just a love story; it is a powerful testament to the endurance of love and the importance of remembering history. With its rich, layered storytelling and deeply moving narrative, *The Sandcastle Girls* is a must-read that will stay with you long after the final page. Bravo, Chris Bohjalian, for crafting such a searing and unforgettable tale.

SHANE SVOREC

Shares How Life's Journey Shapes Stories of Empathy and Resilience

BY ANNA HARLOWE

Shane Svorec's journey as a writer is deeply intertwined with her rich and varied life experiences. Her childhood, marked by constant movement across the country, instilled in her a unique perspective that she channels into her writing. In our interview, Shane discusses how her transient upbringing influenced her narratives, especially in *Broken Little Believer*. She reveals how these experiences fostered adaptability and an appreciation for diversity, elements that are vividly reflected in her literary work.

In *Broken Little Believer*, Shane's personal journey of finding purpose through pain is a poignant exploration of resilience and hope. She opens up about the motivations behind turning her life experiences into a memoir and how the process of writing became a profound tool for healing and self-discovery. Her story is a testament to the strength derived from faith and the relentless pursuit of meaning amidst adversity.

As an independent youth turned foster parent, Shane brings a deeply personal understanding to her advocacy work. Her experiences inform not only her storytelling but also her commitment to fostering resilience and empathy. Shane's insights into the foster system highlight the importance of empathy and support, driving home the message that our origins do not dictate our destiny.

Shane's second book, *The Busy Bridge That Got Its Break*, personifies the Tappan Zee Bridge to tell a heartwarming story that resonates with readers of all ages. Drawing inspiration from her childhood memories, Shane uses the bridge as a metaphor for overlooked individuals who, like the bridge, carry heavy burdens unnoticed. This narrative encourages readers to slow down and appreciate the often-overlooked beauty and struggles around us.

Describing herself as having

Shane Svorec discusses how her transient upbringing, personal challenges, and advocacy work shape her writing, creating stories that foster empathy, resilience, and appreciation for life's simple joys.

the heart of a hippie and the faith of a missionary, Shane's identity manifests vividly in her writing. Her free-spirited love for nature and deep-seated faith shine through, inspiring readers to savor the simple joys of life and approach each day with gratitude and intention. Her works serve as a reminder to pause, appreciate, and connect with the world around us.

Shane's involvement in her community and work in mental health and crisis intervention significantly influence the themes and characters in her books. Her real-world experiences bring authenticity and depth to her writing, allowing her to craft narratives that resonate deeply with readers. Shane's commitment to advocacy and her dedication to uplifting others are evident in every page she writes, making her stories not only compelling but also profoundly impactful.

Through our conversation, it's clear that Shane Svorec's writing is a reflection of her life—rich with experiences, grounded in empathy, and driven by a desire to connect and inspire. Her stories encourage readers to embrace their journeys, find strength in their struggles, and always hold onto hope.

Your upbringing involved traveling across the country and living in numerous places. How has this transient lifestyle influenced your perspective on life, and how does it shape the narratives in your writing, particularly in 'Broken Little Believer?

Moving as frequently as I did as a child and growing up in so many areas, my perspective was formed with the belief that every encounter

and experience can be an opportunity to meet someone special or learn something valuable. Similar to the many places I've lived, my perspective grew broad and flexible. I looked for the beauty in people and places and found appreciation in differences. I learned to be adaptive, outgoing, and patient. As a writer, my upbringing shaped the narratives found in my writing as I strive to use words to paint a picture, offer understanding, and find points of connection. I capture life through the lens of many people and different points of view. I feel an obligation to use my words to create literary works that bring people together and provide a platform for discussion, needed awareness, and greater empathy.

In *Broken Little Believer*, you share your personal journey of finding purpose through pain. What motivated you to turn your life experiences into a book, and how did the process of writing this memoir impact your healing and self-discovery?

As a little girl, whenever something bad happened, I would tell myself there had to be a reason or purpose. I would have crumbled without this habitual internal dialogue and my reliance on faith. We don't survive tragedies if we don't have hope for the future. Without much support, I knew I had to be strong and push myself to keep going. I came to expect that I had to do it alone, and that created a fire within me that I knew I needed to keep lit. As I gained hindsight, I came to see some of the purposes for my pain, and this knowledge reinforced my beliefs. We all endure

hardships at some time or another in our lives, but what we do with the pain and how we choose to live our lives, regardless of it, is a choice we all get to make.

When I faced my own mortality, I knew that the book everyone told me I should write for years couldn't be put off any longer. Tomorrow is not promised to anyone, so I am a proponent of living life and pursuing your dreams now.

As someone who has been both a foster child and a foster parent, how do these experiences inform your advocacy work and the stories you tell? Are there specific messages you hope to convey about resilience and empathy to readers?

Wow! What a great question. My awareness and personal experiences of the foster system motivated me to want to help others. I understood the gaps and limitations of the system and also recognized opportunities to further support those who needed it. When you live through something, you develop greater empathy and understanding. I try to lead by example and use my experiences to form connections rooted in wisdom, patience, and first-hand knowledge. Where we come from or what we endure does not dictate where we go or who we become. I firmly believe that when we know better, we do better.

Your book, *The Busy Bridge That Got Its Break*, personifies a bridge to tell a heartwarming story. What inspired you to write about the Tappan Zee Bridge in this way, and what do you hope readers of all ages take away from this story?

The Tappan Zee Bridge was the backdrop for many of my young memories as a little girl. From my classroom window, I could see the bridge. What always looked like a smile to me because of the way it was designed created within me

Broken Little Believer by Shane Svorec is an inspiring masterpiece that intertwines personal anecdotes with profound life lessons. Svorec's narrative, set against the backdrop of her nomadic childhood in a VW bus, captivates and encourages readers to find purpose amid adversity. This award-winning memoir, celebrated for its raw authenticity and emotional depth, guides readers to embrace pain as a catalyst for growth. A true testament to resilience, Svorec's journey of hope and transformation is both heartwarming and empowering. A must-read for anyone seeking inspiration and a renewed perspective.

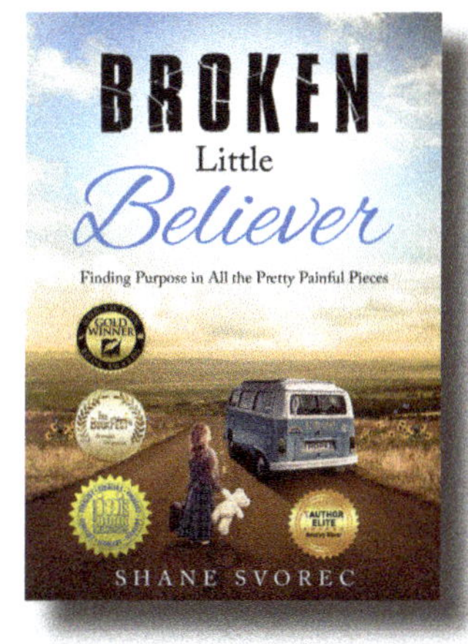

an endearing affection for the bridge. I would get lost staring at it while noticing that the bridge always had vehicles on it day and night. As a child, I wondered when the bridge got a break. As an adult, I viewed the bridge differently but still with affection. As I got older, so did the bridge, and many people wanted to tear it down. The bridge carried much more weight than it was designed to, and it started to break down and look tired. I began to compare people and this "smiling" structure. Like many people, it carried a heavy weight and went unnoticed until a break occurred. Signs were hung from the bridge to prevent people from making permanent decisions in moments of desperation, and emergency phone boxes were placed on the longest bridge in NY should someone in distress need to hear a caring voice. The more I thought about this "smiling" bridge that went unnoticed, the more I drew a parallel between it and the many overlooked people who traveled on it. I wrote this book as a tribute to the bridge, its history, and the lessons it taught me - especially the importance of slowing down to appreciate and value the people, places, and structures around us that often go unnoticed.

You describe yourself as having the heart of a hippie and the faith of a missionary. How do these aspects of your identity manifest in your writing, and how do they help you connect with and inspire your readers?

I am a free-spirited person who loves nature and the everyday beauty of the world. I live with intention and make time to stop and notice things. I am open-minded, a bit of a romantic, and a deep thinker. My zest for life and appreciation for the little things help inspire others to do the same. We live in a busy world, and we are so distracted in our daily lives. I believe my approach to celebrating little moments and savoring simple gifts prompts others to slow down, take a breath, and practice gratitude. When we look at life through a lens of appreciation, we find more things to be grateful for.

As an active member of your community and someone involved in mental health and crisis intervention, how do your real-world experiences and interactions influence the themes and characters in your books? Are there specific stories or lessons from your community work that have found their way into your writing?

I am a cheerleader for the underdog, an advocate for the misunderstood, and a spokesperson for those without a voice. My experiences and awareness of various life challenges have shaped me and fueled my motivation to serve in a way that helps others. I believe we all have strengths, gifts, and talents that can (and should) be used to make a positive difference in the world. Knowing that I can use my own experiences for good and support positive change is gratifying, but it's an obligation we all owe to humanity. We were designed to connect with one another and experience a sense of belonging, value, and purpose. My writing takes many personal and vulnerable experiences and turns them into opportunities to learn and grow from. As a result, my writing encourages others to be true to themselves and unashamed of their pain or past experiences. This is how we live genuinely and lead healthy and fulfilling lives.

PHOTO: Shane Svorec's heartfelt storytelling and profound empathy make her a beacon of inspiration in literature and advocacy.

TRANSFORMING PERSONAL CRISES INTO COMPELLING FICTION

The Resilient Journey of
S.M. STEVENS

S.M. Stevens, acclaimed author and former business executive, whose novels explore complex societal issues with depth and authenticity.

BY BEN ALAN

S.M. Stevens transitioned from business writing to fiction after health crises, creating novels that tackle societal issues with strong female protagonists and authentic, thought-provoking narratives.

S.M. Stevens' journey to becoming a fiction writer is as compelling as the narratives she crafts. A seasoned business writer with a robust career in corporate communications, Stevens found her true calling in fiction through a series of unexpected life events. Her transition from the boardroom to the writer's desk was catalyzed by two significant health crises, which provided her the time and impetus to explore her creative side.

After a severe horseback riding accident left her with a broken pelvis, Stevens turned to writing as a means of coping with her temporary immobility. This period of enforced rest resulted in her first middle-grade novel, "Shannon's Odyssey," written for her animal-loving daughter. Almost a year later, a diagnosis of ovarian cancer and the subsequent chemotherapy sessions gave her the opportunity to pen "Bit Players, Has-Been Actors and Other Posers," a novel aimed at musical theatre-loving teens, including her older daughter.

Stevens' writing career, born out of personal adversity, has since flourished. Her first adult novel, "Horseshoes and Hand Grenades," was inspired by the #metoo movement and explores the parallels between workplace sexual harassment and childhood incest. Her

S.M. Stevens masterfully blends compelling storytelling with profound societal insights, creating unforgettable characters and narratives that resonate deeply.

upcoming novel, "Beautiful and Terrible Things," set for release in summer 2024, delves into themes of friendship, mental illness, and social justice, reflecting her commitment to addressing complex societal issues through her fiction.

In addition to her literary achievements, Stevens has had a distinguished business career, holding executive positions at Fortune 500 companies and nonprofit organizations. Her extensive experience in corporate communications has undoubtedly influenced her approach to writing, teaching her the discipline to write amidst constant interruptions and the ability to convey powerful messages succinctly.

Stevens' novels are known for their strong female protagonists and their exploration of challenging circumstances, offering readers both entertainment and thought-provoking content. Her dedication to authenticity and representation in literature is evident in her meticulous research and the use of sensitivity readers to ensure diverse and accurate portrayals of her characters.

As Stevens continues to write and inspire, her story serves as a testament to the resilience of the human spirit and the transformative power of storytelling. Your novels often tackle complex societal issues such as workplace harassment and mental health struggles. What drives you to explore these topics, and how do you balance entertainment value with the exploration of serious subjects?

While I love a good escapist beach read on occasion, I'm more drawn to fiction that challenges me in some way. So that's what I write. Complex themes provide ample room to explore and provoke thought. As for balancing entertainment, that's easy: simply portray life as we know it, which is, hopefully, filled with humor, light and love as well as challenges and tragedy.

Your upcoming novel, Beautiful and Terrible Things, delves into themes of friendship, mental illness, and social justice in a contemporary American setting. What inspired this story, and what message do you hope readers will take away from it?

I wanted to depict contemporary society realistically, and that meant including multiple social ills rather than highlighting one. I am pleased when my younger readers confirm, "Yep, that's life in a big city today."

I hope readers, regardless of their views on each issue, put down the book with a greater empathy for the real people that exist behind the statistics. And I hope I inspire people to get more involved in the causes important to them, by showing the various paths, large and small, that my characters take toward greater activism.

Your extensive career in business includes executive positions at Fortune 500 companies and non-profit organizations. How has your background in corporate communications informed your approach to writing fiction?

The greatest impact my communications career had on my fiction-writing career was teaching me how to write with constant interruptions. I learned to write in five-minute increments—literally, and to not lose focus, despite multiple interruptions from my staff and my boss. That carried over to interruptions from the family and the dogs when writing at home.

Your novel Horseshoes and Hand Grenades depicts both childhood sexual abuse and workplace sexual harassment. What drove you to merge those topics in one narrative?

I had a draft of a novel about a woman dealing with "mild" incest, sitting on my shelf. When the #metoo movement took off, I was fascinated at how society asks the same questions of harassment victims as it does of incest survivors; questions such as: Why did you wait so long to speak up? What's your ulterior motive in speaking up now? Was it really that bad? The novel attempts to answer those questions (which, when you think about it, are never posed to victims of other crimes).

Your novels often feature strong female protagonists navigating challenging circumstances. Can you speak to the importance of representation in literature, and how do you ensure authenticity and depth in portraying diverse characters and their experiences?

Representation, and cultural appropriation, are very important topics. All any author can do in an effort to be authentic is to research, research, research—not only reading but talking to people, and then draw on our understanding of human nature to craft three-dimensional, believable characters. Having a multitude of sensitivity readers, as I did, is also critical. I drew on the experiences and insights of others in the areas of mental health, race, gender, sexuality and immigration to inform Beautiful and Terrible Things. I even found a Filipino artist to offer feedback on one character!

The Bit Players series was inspired by your daughter's love for musical theatre. How did your personal experiences as a parent influence the creation of these stories, and what challenges did you face in writing for a younger audience?

I participated in high school and college drama, and then volunteered at my daughters' school theatre program. Those experiences are reflected in the Bit Players series. The biggest challenge was to not embarrass my teenaged daughter; it was for her I came up with my pen name, so her friends wouldn't find out that her mother wrote about teens behaving badly. (She is now a mature and astute writer herself, and no longer ashamed of our connection.)

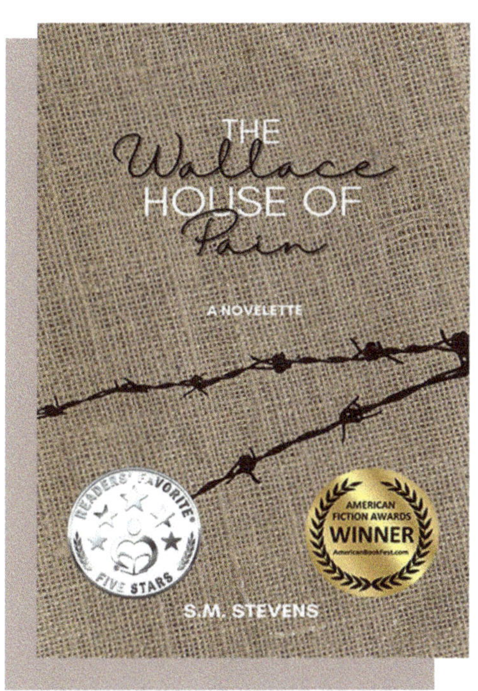

The Wallace House of Pain: A Novelette by S.M. Stevens is a compelling exploration of strained family dynamics and modern social justice issues. Winner of the 2023 American Fiction Award and the Chanticleer International Book Award First Prize, this work delves into the tumultuous relationship between activist Xander Wallace and his conservative father, Jim. Stevens masterfully portrays the palpable tension and awkwardness that define their interactions, making readers feel Xander's discomfort and his stepmother's desperate attempts to bond. The novelette's powerful message of acceptance and love resonates deeply, highlighting the struggles of living authentically in the face of societal and familial pressures. With its rich character study and emotional depth, 'The Wallace House of Pain' is a short but profoundly impactful read that leaves a lasting impression. Highly recommended for those seeking a thoughtful and touching narrative.

Unveiling the Literary Brilliance of
MICHELLE M. PILLOW
Inviting Readers Into Her Enchanting Worlds

BY BEN F. ONCU

Michelle M. Pillow, New York Times and USA Today bestselling author, discusses her diverse genres, creative process, and global impact, inviting readers into her enchanting worlds.

In the realm of literature, there are storytellers who possess a unique gift: the ability to transport readers to worlds beyond imagination, where love, mystery, and adventure intertwine. Michelle M. Pillow stands as one such luminary, a beacon of creativity whose literary endeavors have captured the hearts of millions. In our exclusive interview with this esteemed author, we delve into the depths of her prolific career, exploring the genesis of her storytelling prowess and the boundless realms she creates.

With over a million books sold, Michelle M. Pillow has carved a remarkable niche in the literary landscape, earning accolades as a New York Times and USA TODAY bestselling author. Renowned for her mastery of romance and mystery, Pillow's narratives are imbued with rich world-building that serves as portals for the imagination. Whether it's the enchanting allure of the Qurilixen World, the intrigue of the Warlocks MacGregor series, or the magical realms of the Order of Magic series, Pillow's tales captivate readers with their gripping narratives and vibrant characters.

Evangeline Anderson, herself a luminary in the literary world, extols Pillow's work, describing it as a seamless fusion of curiosity and passion, where investigative reporters collide with hot Alien Dragon-Shifters in a symphony of excitement and romance. Tasha Black echoes this sentiment, praising Pillow's ability to infuse her novels with humor and heat, creating a tapestry of emotions that resonates deeply with readers.

But what lies behind the veil of Pillow's creative process? In our interview, she offers a glimpse into the inner workings of her mind, revealing the meticulous craftsmanship that goes into crafting each tale. From

Continued *on page 12*

"Michelle M. Pillow captivates with rich storytelling, vibrant characters, and unparalleled creativity, earning accolades as a literary luminary.

← **Continued** *from page 10*

the inception of characters to the intricacies of world-building, Pillow's approach is a testament to her dedication to the craft.

Yet, amidst the accolades and acclaim, Pillow remains grounded, attributing her success to a relentless pursuit of excellence and an unwavering commitment to her readers. With sage advice for aspiring writers and a profound appreciation for the global reach of her stories, Pillow's humility shines through, reminding us of the profound impact of literature on the human experience.

As we embark on this journey into the realms of Michelle M. Pillow's imagination, we invite you to immerse yourself in the magic of storytelling, where worlds are born from words, and dreams take flight on the wings of imagination. Join us as we unravel the mysteries, explore the depths of love, and embark on adventures beyond the realms of possibility. Welcome to the enchanting world of Michelle M. Pillow.

You write in many different romance genres. What drew you to writing romance and what do you enjoy most about it?

I want to create unforgettable, emotional tales. My goal is to write stories that not only entertain but also linger in the hearts and minds of readers long after the final page has been turned. I want readers to become fully immersed and read themselves into the story, whether it's to agree or disagree with the characters. Seeing characters deal with problems (even dealing with them poorly) helps us to navigate our own issues. Romance does all this and more.

Having written in many romance genres, one thing became obvious very quickly: for better or worse, I wasn't a one-genre writer. My muse likes to explore and research, so I let her. I'm fortunate to have readers who follow me from genre to genre.

How do you come up with ideas and stories for your many series featuring shifters, aliens, ghosts, etc.?

Character and world-building are my favorite parts of writing. Whether the world is a modern city or a faraway planet, my cha-

racters are products of where they come from. I start with character history and personality quirks. Once I know those, I know what kind of adult they are and how they might react to the situations I put them in. I need to know their needs and motivations. Physical attributes are usually the last thing I think about.

What is your writing process like? Take us through a typical day when you are working on a new book.

Working as a professional author means deadlines. Lots and lots of deadlines. Normally, I'll have books being promoted, another in writing/edits, another in planning stages, and then there is the admin and marketing. It's a never-ending cycle.

I work anywhere. Not because I've wanted to over the years, but because I had to—waiting rooms, parking lots, airports, hotels. I even finished a book in the passenger seat of a car while driving halfway across the country. It wasn't a fun 10 hours for the driver. LOL Luckily for me, he still married me.

How do you come up with the unique worlds and settings for your stories? Do you draw inspiration from real-life locations or completely imagine them?

It's a combination of imagination and inspiration.

Doing things away from the computer can help to refill the creative well. Often, that's when the best ideas strike—when you're not looking for them. Experiencing something makes you better versed in writing about it—not that I can take off into spaceships, but I can tour a ghost town, or interview an expert in paranormal investigations about their techniques, or visit museums.

You're bound to learn something every time you step out into the world.

You have a significant number of series and books to your name. How do you keep track of the different worlds and characters you've created?

It can be difficult, especially when it's in a series I haven't written in for years. I think it's a matter of knowing my worlds and characters, like you'd know a friend or the house you grew

up in. Sometimes my mind can walk right back into that room, or palace, or ship and see it because my imagination has already spent time there. And, less fun of an answer, I rely on my series bibles and notes to fill in the gaps.

Do you have a favorite series or character that you have created? Which one and why?

Romance Writers of America recognized me for publishing over 100 books. Out of those, it's hard to pick a favorite. I'm blessed to have a career that allows me to visit many different worlds. My first book, a Gothic Regency, Forget Me Not (formerly The Mists of Midnight) will always hold a special place in my heart because it's what started my career.

I'm best known for books that fall under the Qurilixen world sci-fi umbrella—there are shifters, aliens, and space pirates. I like the Realm Immortal series for the vast world building and the big cast of characters. It's like an adult fairytale. I like the Tribes of the Vampire series because I'm a horror genre fan, and those books have darker themes.

One theme that runs through several of my series is the idea of family. Warlocks MacGregor series is a prime example. They're a

SAMPLING OF AWARDS & NOTABLES

- New York Times Bestselling Author

- USA Today Bestselling Author

- Millions of books sold

- Recognized for having 100 Published Romances (RWA)

- #1 Amazon.com Bestselling Author

- Bestseller at Apple Books, Kobo, Nook, Googleplay

- Romantic Times BOOKreviews Magazine

- Lifetime Achievement Award Nominee 2011

- Winner 2006 Romantic Times Bookclub Magazine's Reviewer's Choice

- Award for the historical romance Maiden and the Monster

- 2007 Romantic Times Bookclub Magazine's Reviewer's Choice Award

- Nominee for the futuristic romance The Bound Prince

- Kensington Brava Novella Contest Finalist (3rd)

- 2015 Virginia Romance Writers HOLT Medallion Award of Merit

recipient for outstanding literary fiction in Paranormal, Love Potions

- Refugee Extra on SyFy's Z Nations, Season 3, Fall 2016

- Mississippi Arts Commission (MAC) 2022 Grant Recipient

- Amazon Direct Publishing's KDP University @ Home with Michelle M. Pillow – Webinar discussing book marketing, publishing, branding, and writing in multiple genres.

PHOTO: *With over a million books sold, Michelle M. Pillow has carved a remarkable niche in the literary landscape, earning accolades as a New York Times and USA TODAY bestselling author.*

(Photos courtesy of Michelle M. Pillow)

close-knit family of mischievous immortals living in modern-day Wisconsin. They might not always get along, but they'll protect each other until the end… but not without a few pranks in the process.

What advice would you give to aspiring romance writers?

There is no magic pill. You must do the research and the work. Well, coffee is kind of like magic, and energy helps do the research, so maybe that's my secret. LOL

Research everything—your book, marketing, promo, your genre—and think about the long-term goals, not just instant career gratification.

Most importantly: Write the book. No book, no reason to go through the trouble of everything else. The book is the fun part!

Your books have been translated into other languages. What's it like seeing your stories reach global audiences?

I remember when a publisher first sent me the first Japanese translation of my book. I still have it on my shelf, along with the translations that came after. I was so excited I made everyone look at it. As an author, I want to make readers experience something. To know that people on the other side of the world that I never met and whose language I can't speak are being entertained by something I created is… there are no words.

How much research goes into your books, especially when they involve elements of history, mythology, or science fiction?

I confess, sometimes I'll plot a book because I want to research a topic. It's so easy to get lost in that part of the process. I always want to be learning. With historicals, I can get lost in the anthropological details of how people lived. There is so much to think about—where did they sleep, how did they interact, how did they cook, what is their political climate? The list is endless.

People don't always realize that fantasy and futuristic books also take research. I often base my futuristic worlds on historical societies. Even if the readers don't see it, it helps ground the worlds in something familiar and gives them context. With futuristics, I need to know about space travel or tech. Not all research makes it onto the pages, but it does inform the overall feel of the story.

What is your favorite part of writing?

World building. I love taking all my research, experiences, and imagination and making something out of it.

Also, the feeling when I complete a book, knowing that everything in front of me is because I did something, I created that world. And the best is when the book is released and I start hearing from readers who loved reading it as much as I loved writing it.

Why are books important?

Books provide entertainment, teach us things, and take us on fantastic journeys. Reading lets us absorb thoughts and ideas that we might not have otherwise considered. Maybe most profound is the way, during hard times like the pandemic, fiction can give a much-needed form of escapism.

What are you like in person?

I'm told I'm quirky and adventurous. I'm not adventurous in the sense you'll find me hanging off the top of Everest, but I'm willing to try new things and am always open to new opportunities. I've been on paranormal investigations of museums and vaudeville theatres. I was an extra on Z Nation. I've climbed Mayan temples in Belize. I'd say quirky because it seems to describe my sense of humor. I'm also a giant paranormal/sci-fi nerd, and proud of it.

I feel privileged to be an author, to be able to do a job I love, and that readers are willing to give my books a chance. Writing is such a personal experience, and to be able to share an emotional journey with others is amazing.

Thank you for having me!

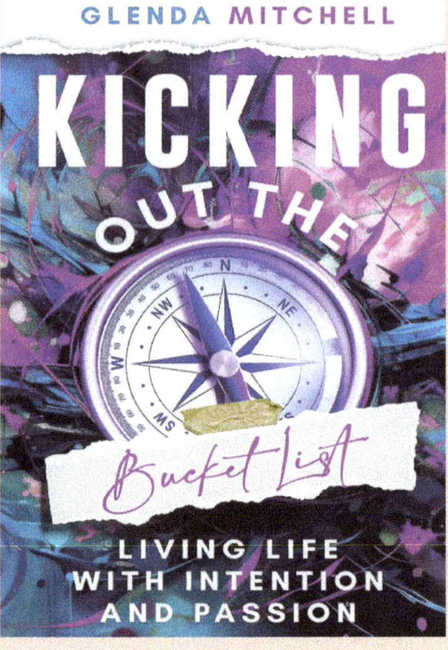

WELL, THAT WAS UNEXPECTED

by Jesse Q. Sutanto

Well, That Was Unexpected is a hilarious, heartwarming tale of love, family, and cultural discovery, beautifully crafted by Sutanto.

Well, That Was Unexpected by Jesse Q. Sutanto is a delightful and uproarious journey that captures the essence of young love, cultural exploration, and the chaos of family meddling. Sutanto, known for her witty storytelling, delivers yet another gem with this young adult rom-com that is as heartwarming as it is hilarious.

The story follows Sharlot Citra, a teenager from LA who is abruptly transported to Indonesia after her mother catches her in an embarrassing situation. The plan is to reconnect with her roots, but Sharlot soon finds herself entangled in a scheme far more complicated than she anticipated. Enter George Clooney Tanuwijaya, the son of one of Indonesia's wealthiest families, whose father is equally determined to guide his son's romantic life. The twist? Their parents have been impersonating them online, setting them up for a relationship neither of them wanted.

Sutanto masterfully crafts a narrative that is both laugh-out-loud funny and deeply touching. The cultural backdrop of Indonesia is painted with vibrant detail, offering readers a rich tapestry of traditions, landscapes, and familial bonds. The chemistry between Sharlot and George is electric, evolving from initial reluctance to a genuine connection that surprises them both. Their journey is filled with witty banter, awkward encounters, and moments of introspection that make their relationship feel authentic and relatable.

What truly sets this novel apart is its exploration of family dynamics. Sutanto captures the essence of meddlesome yet well-meaning parents with humor and empathy, highlighting the universal struggle of balancing familial expectations with personal desires. The parents' antics, while outrageous, are rooted in love, adding depth to the comedic elements of the story.

Well, That Was Unexpected is a charming love letter to Indonesia and the complexities of growing up in a multicultural world. Sutanto's ability to blend humor with heartfelt moments makes this book a standout in the YA genre. It's a story about finding love in the most unexpected places and learning to embrace the chaos that comes with it. Whether you're a fan of rom-coms or simply looking for a feel-good read, this novel is sure to leave you smiling long after the final page.

SOLDIERS, TEMPLES, AND CRYSTALS

by Terry Overton

An enthralling adventure that brilliantly intertwines history and faith, making ancient stories come alive for readers of all ages.

Soldiers, Temples, and Crystals is a captivating start to The Newton Chronicles series, blending adventure, history, and biblical intrigue in a way that is both engaging and thought-provoking. Terry Overton, with the artistic contributions of Christopher Jackson, crafts a narrative that is sure to appeal to readers who enjoy a mix of mystery and historical exploration.

The story kicks off with a compelling premise: Luke Alexander's father is missing, and while the world presumes him dead, Luke believes otherwise. This sets the stage for a thrilling adventure as Luke, along with his friends Nathan and Lydia, embarks on a quest that intertwines with the mysteries of Isaac Newton and the legendary Solomon's temple. The trio's dynamic is one of the highlights of the book, with each character bringing unique skills and perspectives to their journey. Nathan's background as a pastor's kid and Lydia's linguistic talents add depth and diversity to their interactions and problem-solving approaches.

Overton does an excellent job of weaving historical and biblical elements into the narrative, making these ancient stories feel vibrant and relevant. The inclusion of a mysterious watch and cryptic notes adds layers of intrigue that keep the reader engaged and eager to uncover the truth alongside the protagonists. The pacing is well-balanced, with enough action to keep younger readers hooked, while also providing moments of reflection and insight that will resonate with older audiences.

One of the book's strengths is its ability to make history and the Bible come alive. Overton's storytelling invites readers to see these ancient tales through a new lens, sparking curiosity and encouraging further exploration of the historical and spiritual themes presented. The adventure is not just a physical journey but also a quest for truth and understanding, which adds a meaningful dimension to the story.

Soldiers, Temples, and Crystals is a delightful adventure that will captivate readers of all ages. It's a story that not only entertains but also inspires curiosity about history and faith. As the first installment in The Newton Chronicles, it sets a strong foundation for what promises to be an exciting series. Whether you're a fan of historical mysteries, biblical tales, or simply a good adventure, this book is sure to satisfy.

INDEPENDENCE

by Christopher C Tubbs

A transformative guide that inspires intentional living, celebrating personal achievements, and pursuing genuine joy beyond societal expectations. Highly motivating read!

Kicking Out The Bucket List: Living Life With Intention And Passion by Glenda Mitchell is a thought-provoking guide that encourages readers to redefine their approach to life. Instead of adhering to a traditional bucket list filled with societal expectations, Mitchell advocates for a more introspective and personalized journey.

The book is rooted in Mitchell's own transformative experiences, particularly her near-death encounter with a severe blood clot in 2016. This pivotal moment led her to reassess her life priorities, prompting her to focus on what truly mattered to her. Through this lens, she shares stories of her adventures and the lessons she learned along the way, offering readers both entertainment and inspiration.

Mitchell's narrative is designed to motivate individuals to take control of their lives by making intentional choices that align with their core values. She emphasizes the importance of celebrating personal achievements and recognizing the richness of experiences already lived, rather than constantly seeking the next big goal.

The book challenges readers to disrupt their routines and consider what brings genuine joy and fulfillment. It encourages them to craft a life that reflects their unique desires and passions, rather than conforming to external pressures or expectations. By doing so, readers can find deeper meaning and satisfaction in their lives.

Overall, *"Kicking Out The Bucket List"* serves as a reminder that true success and happiness come from pursuing what is personally significant and valuable, ultimately leading to a life lived with intention and passion.

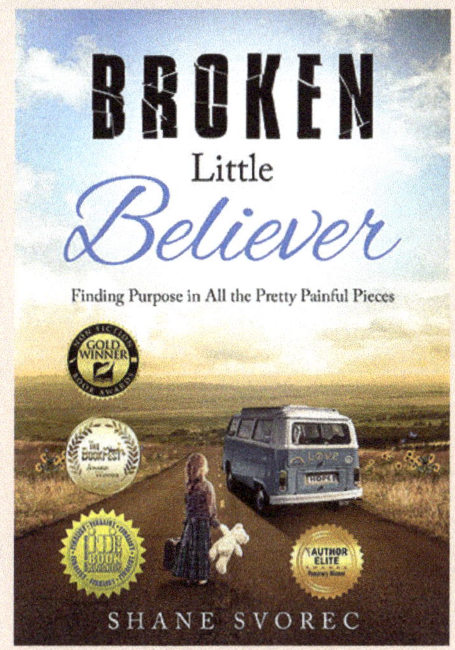

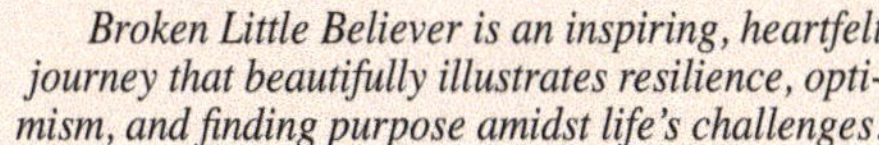

BROKEN LITTLE BELIEVER
by Shane Svorec

A LOVE TO DIE FOR
by Joseph Seechack

EMPOWERED WOMAN
by Adebola Ajao

Broken Little Believer is an inspiring, heartfelt journey that beautifully illustrates resilience, optimism, and finding purpose amidst life's challenges.

Broken Little Believer is an inspiring, heartfelt journey that beautifully illustrates resilience, optimism, and finding purpose amidst life's challenges.

Broken Little Believer by Shane Svorec is a captivating memoir that blends personal anecdotes with universal lessons of resilience and optimism. An award-winning and critically acclaimed book, it takes readers on an intimate journey through Svorec's transient upbringing, experienced from the back seat of a VW bus, highlighting her empathetic spirit and perpetual optimism.

Svorec's narrative is deeply engaging, offering a refreshing perspective on overcoming adversity. Her ability to find purpose in pain and her refusal to be a victim of her circumstances provide a powerful message of hope. The book's structure, interweaving true stories with profound reflections, makes it both a compelling memoir and a guide to personal growth.

This memoir stands out for its authenticity and relatability. Svorec shares her experiences with such openness that readers are encouraged to reflect on their own lives. Themes of adaptability, gratitude, and purposeful living are seamlessly integrated into the narrative, making it a source of inspiration for anyone seeking to navigate their challenges.

Broken Little Believer is more than just a collection of stories; it's a roadmap to finding peace and fulfillment in a chaotic world. Svorec's journey demonstrates how uncomfortable experiences can lead to self-exploration and growth, fostering a healthy perspective and an attitude of gratitude. Her ability to connect with others and uncover profound, purposeful connections along her path adds depth to her tale.

Whether you're feeling lost or simply seeking inspiration, this book offers a renewed sense of hope and belief in the possibilities that lie ahead. Shane Svorec's story is a testament to the strength of the human spirit and the transformative power of resilience.

"A Love to Die For" beautifully captures love, loss, and healing, offering a heartfelt journey through grief and resilience.

Joseph Seechack's *A Love to Die For"* is a poignant exploration of love, loss, and the arduous journey of healing. The novel opens with the idyllic marriage of Ron and Grace Butler, a couple whose love story seems to have been plucked from the pages of a romance novel. However, the sudden and tragic death of Ron shatters this perfect world, leaving Grace and their children in a state of profound grief.

Seechack masterfully captures the raw emotions that accompany such a devastating loss. Grace's journey through the stages of grief is depicted with authenticity and sensitivity, making her struggles relatable to anyone who has experienced the loss of a loved one. The author delves deep into Grace's psyche, exploring her feelings of emptiness, anger, and despair, while also highlighting the strength and resilience that gradually emerge as she navigates her new reality.

One of the novel's strengths is its portrayal of the support system that surrounds Grace. Friends and family play a crucial role in her healing process, offering a sense of community and understanding that is both heartwarming and inspiring. Seechack emphasizes the importance of leaning on others during times of hardship, a message that resonates throughout the book.

The narrative is beautifully written, with Seechack's prose capturing the essence of both love and loss. The flashbacks to Ron and Grace's life together are particularly moving, serving as a reminder of the enduring power of love even in the face of tragedy. These moments provide a stark contrast to Grace's present reality, underscoring the depth of her loss while also celebrating the love that continues to shape her life.

A Love to Die For is a touching and thought-provoking read that will resonate with anyone who has experienced the complexities of grief. Joseph Seechack has crafted a story that is both heart-wrenching and uplifting, reminding us of the enduring power of love and the resilience of the human spirit. This book is a testament to the strength it takes to navigate the darkest moments of life and emerge stronger on the other side.

Empowered Woman is an inspiring, practical guide that equips women to unlock potential and confidently achieve their life goals.

Empowered Woman by Adebola Ajao is a transformative guide that speaks directly to the heart of every woman striving to reach her full potential. With a stellar 4.8 out of 5 stars from 34 ratings, this Kindle edition is a must-read for any professional woman feeling stuck or uncertain about her next steps.

Adebola Ajao, a professional, wife, and mother of three, skillfully intertwines her personal experiences with actionable advice, making the book both relatable and practical. The five principles she outlines—Thinking Big, Conquering Your Fears, Seeking and Acquiring Knowledge, Finding Mentors, and Acting and Following Through—are not just theoretical concepts but are broken down into easy-to-follow steps that can be seamlessly integrated into daily life.

What sets this book apart is its focus on empowerment through practical application. Ajao provides readers with the tools to discover hidden talents, shift mindsets, and dismantle self-doubt. Her approach is both motivational and pragmatic, ensuring that readers not only feel inspired but are also equipped to take tangible steps toward their goals.

The testimonials from other readers echo the book's impact. Many praise its inspirational nature and the way it redefines familiar principles to resonate with modern women. The action-oriented guidance is particularly highlighted, with readers appreciating the step-by-step approach that accommodates even the busiest of schedules.

Overall, *Empowered Woman* is more than just a book; it's a roadmap to self-discovery and achievement. Whether you're looking to advance in your career, improve personal relationships, or embark on a new venture, this book offers the insights and encouragement needed to embark on a self-empowering journey. Download your copy today and take the first step toward maximizing your potential and building your legacy.

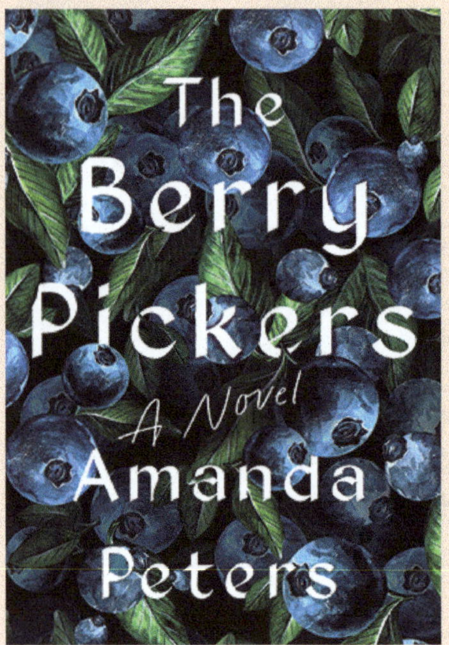

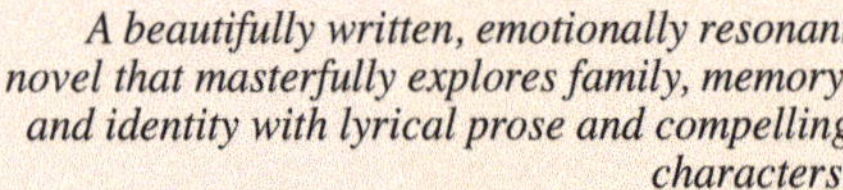

THE BERRY PICKERS
by Amanda Peters

UTOPIA FALLING
by R.C. Vielee

ESCAPING MY DEMONS
by Joseph Fagarazzi

A beautifully written, emotionally resonant novel that masterfully explores family, memory, and identity with lyrical prose and compelling characters.

The Berry Pickers by Amanda Peters is a deeply moving novel that explores themes of family, memory, and identity. Set in the 1960s, the story begins with Joe, bedridden and reflecting on his life, particularly the day his sister Ruthie went missing. This event serves as the emotional core of the novel, affecting Joe and his family profoundly.

Peters excels in character development, particularly with Joe, who is portrayed with a mix of vulnerability and strength. His relationships with his sister Mae, brother Ben, and mother are depicted with nuance, highlighting the complexities of familial bonds. The novel also provides a vivid portrayal of the socio-economic challenges faced by migrant workers from Nova Scotia, who come to Maine for the berry-picking season.

The writing is lyrical and immersive, with Peters' descriptions of the landscape capturing both its beauty and harshness. The dialogue is authentic, and the characters' voices are distinct and believable. The novel's themes of loss, resilience, and the search for identity are explored with sensitivity and depth.

The Berry Pickers is a compelling read that offers a window into a specific time and place while addressing universal themes. It is recommended for readers who enjoy character-driven stories with rich historical settings. Amanda Peters has crafted a story that is both heart-wrenching and hopeful, making it a memorable addition to contemporary fiction.

The Berry Pickers leaves a lasting impression, making it a must-read for those interested in the complexities of family relationships and the enduring impact of past events.

"Utopia Falling: A Darkness Rises" captivates with its rich world-building, compelling characters, and thought-provoking exploration of utopia's fragility. Engaging read!

Utopia Falling by R.C. Vielee is an intriguing entry into the realm of dark epic fantasy, setting the stage for what promises to be a captivating saga. The novel introduces readers to the contrasting worlds of Tartica and Evidar, each with its own unique challenges and philosophies. Vielee's world-building is commendable, painting a vivid picture of a near-utopian society on the brink of chaos and a parallel realm shrouded in perpetual darkness.

The protagonist, Reyne, is a relatable character whose simple dreams are upended by forces beyond his control. His journey from a hopeful groom-to-be to a reluctant hero is compelling, and readers will find themselves rooting for him as he grapples with the weight of his newfound responsibilities. The tension between Reyne's disbelief in the existence of Evidar and the undeniable reality of its threat adds an interesting layer to the narrative.

Vielee's exploration of human nature and the fragility of utopia is thought-provoking, raising questions about the sustainability of ideal societies in the face of ambition and greed. The novel's central theme — that utopia cannot withstand the onslaught of human nature — resonates throughout the story, providing a solid foundation for the unfolding drama.

However, while the premise is strong, the execution occasionally falters. Some plot developments feel rushed, and certain character motivations could benefit from deeper exploration. The pacing, at times, is uneven, with moments of intense action interspersed with slower sections that may test the reader's patience.

The antagonists, particularly the Devil's Blacksmith, are intriguing but could be further fleshed out to enhance their impact on the story. Understanding their motivations and backstories in greater detail would add depth to the conflict and heighten the stakes.

Overall, *Utopia Falling: A Darkness Rises* is a promising start to the Utopia Falling Saga. R.C. Vielee has crafted a world rich with potential, and while there are areas for improvement, the novel lays a solid foundation for the continuation of the series. Fans of dark fantasy will find much to enjoy here, and with further development, the saga could become a standout in the genre. I look forward to seeing how the story evolves in the next installment.

Joseph Fagarazzi's 'Escaping My Demons' is a multi-award-winning memoir of resilience, offering profound inspiration through his journey from adversity to triumph.

Joseph Fagarazzi's memoir, *Escaping My Demons*, is a poignant narrative that chronicles a harrowing journey from profound neglect and abuse to eventual triumph and healing. From his earliest days in Venice, Italy, where he was left in a convent while his parents sought a new life in London, Joseph paints a vivid picture of relentless emotional and physical torment inflicted upon him by his own father.

The book unfolds with raw honesty, recounting how Joseph endured relentless criticism and belittlement, all the while yearning desperately for parental love that never materialized. His father's constant reminders that he was unwanted and a mistake left lasting scars, shaping Joseph's belief that he was destined for failure.

Yet, amid the darkness of his upbringing, Joseph discovers resilience. He shares how he found strength to overcome his demons, redefine his self-worth, and carve out a successful path for himself in Australia. From managing clothing stores to venturing into property development and real estate, each chapter in his life is a testament to perseverance and determination.

Escaping My Demons not only serves as a powerful memoir of survival but also as a beacon of hope for those facing similar adversities. Joseph's journey from victim to victor is a compelling narrative of transformation, demonstrating that with inner resolve and a shift in perspective, one can rise above even the most daunting challenges. His story resonates deeply, inspiring readers to confront their own demons and find healing and purpose in their lives.

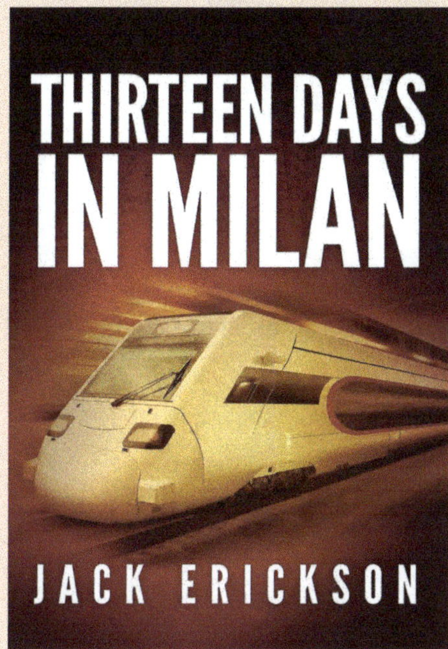

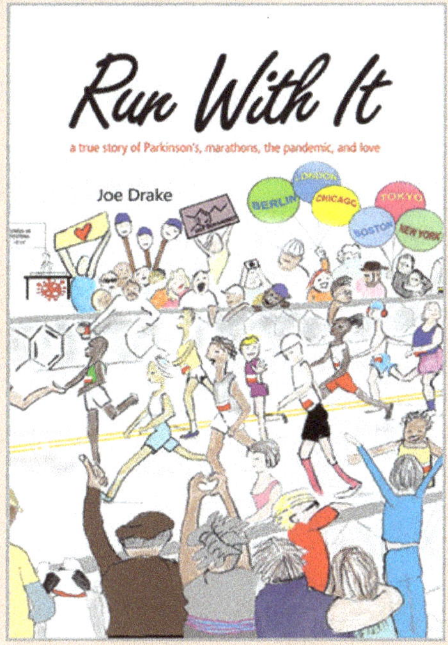

THIRTEEN DAYS IN MILAN
by Thirteen Days in Milan

RUN WITH IT
by Joe Drake

THIS IS WHY WE LIED
by Adebola Ajao

Thirteen Days in Milan is a thrilling, fast-paced adventure with compelling characters and suspenseful twists that keep readers hooked..

Thirteen Days in Milan by Jack Erickson is a gripping political assassination romance thriller that keeps readers on the edge of their seats from start to finish. The story follows Sylvia de Matteo, an American commercial photographer and single mother, who finds herself in a terrifying situation when she is taken hostage by terrorists during a political assassination at Milan's bustling Stazione Centrale.

Erickson masterfully weaves a tale of suspense and intrigue as Sylvia is thrust into a world of danger and uncertainty. The plot is fast-paced, with plenty of twists and turns that keep the reader guessing. The tension is palpable as Sylvia's captors discover her father's wealth and demand a ransom, setting off a race against time for Milan's anti-terrorism police, DIGOS, to rescue her.

The characters are well-developed, with Sylvia emerging as a strong and resilient protagonist. Her determination to survive and reunite with her daughter adds an emotional depth to the story that resonates with readers. The dynamic between Sylvia and the terrorist leader is particularly intriguing, as it explores themes of trust and deception in a high-stakes environment.

Erickson's vivid descriptions of Milan and the Italian Alps provide a rich backdrop for the unfolding drama, immersing readers in the setting and enhancing the overall reading experience. The author's attention to detail and ability to create a sense of place is commendable.

While the book has received mixed reviews due to previous editing errors, it's important to note that these issues have been addressed and corrected in the current ebook edition. The story itself is compelling and well worth the read for fans of the thriller genre.

Overall, *Thirteen Days in Milan* is an engaging and thrilling read that combines elements of political intrigue, romance, and suspense. It's a solid start to the Milan Thriller Series and leaves readers eager to explore the subsequent books. If you're looking for a captivating thriller with a strong female lead, this book is definitely worth adding to your reading list.

"Run With It" is an inspiring, humourous, and deeply moving memoir of resilience, community support, and triumph over adversity. Highly recommended!

Run With It by Joe Drake is an inspiring memoir that captures an extraordinary journey of resilience and determination. At 60, newly diagnosed with Parkinson's disease, Drake sets out to conquer all six World Marathon Majors within six weeks, a challenge intensified by the COVID-19 pandemic's impact on race schedules.

Drake's writing is a delightful blend of humor and insight, drawing readers into the exhilarating highs and challenging lows of marathon running. His narrative is both informative and entertaining, making the complex logistics and intense physical demands of such an undertaking accessible and engaging. Beyond running, the memoir highlights the importance of a supportive network of friends, family, and fellow runners in empowering someone to face daunting challenges head-on.

The book excels in portraying Drake's personal growth and the strategies he develops to manage Parkinson's. His story is a testament to human perseverance and the power of community. Vivid descriptions of each marathon, coupled with Drake's candid reflections, offer an inspiring perspective on overcoming adversity.

Run With It is a must-read for anyone interested in running, battling chronic illness, or simply appreciating a heartfelt tale of triumph against the odds. Drake's debut as an author is nothing short of remarkable, leaving readers both moved and motivated. His story encourages us to confront our own challenges with courage and to find inspiration in the journeys of others. Whether you are a seasoned marathoner or someone facing your own personal battles, Drake's memoir offers valuable lessons in perseverance, hope, and the enduring human spirit.

A masterful thriller with gripping suspense, intricate plot twists, and compelling characters that keep you hooked from start to finish.

Karin Slaughter's *This Is Why We Lied* is a masterful addition to the Will Trent series, delivering a gripping murder mystery that keeps readers on the edge of their seats from start to finish. As the twelfth book in the series, it continues to showcase Slaughter's exceptional talent for crafting intricate plots filled with suspense, complex characters, and unexpected twists.

Set against the eerie backdrop of McAlpine Lodge, an off-the-grid mountaintop retreat, the novel begins with what should be a romantic honeymoon for GBI investigator Will Trent and medical examiner Sara Linton. However, the tranquility is shattered by a blood-curdling scream, leading to the discovery of the lodge manager, Mercy McAlpine, dead. With a storm raging and the only road washed out, the tension escalates as it becomes clear that the murderer is among the guests.

Slaughter expertly weaves a tale of deception and intrigue, where every character harbors secrets and everyone is a suspect. The isolated setting amplifies the suspense, creating a claustrophobic atmosphere that heightens the stakes. As Will and Sara delve deeper into the lives of the McAlpine family and the other guests, they uncover a tangled web of lies and hidden motives, making it increasingly difficult to discern friend from foe.

The novel's strength lies in its well-developed characters, particularly the dynamic between Will and Sara. Their relationship adds depth to the narrative, providing moments of tenderness amidst the chaos. Slaughter's ability to balance personal drama with the overarching mystery is commendable, making the characters relatable and their struggles palpable.

This Is Why We Lied is a must-read for fans of the Will Trent series and anyone who enjoys a well-crafted thriller. With its engaging storyline, atmospheric setting, and memorable characters, it solidifies Karin Slaughter's reputation as a master storyteller. Whether you're a longtime fan or new to the series, this book is sure to leave you eagerly anticipating the next installment.

Jack Erickson discusses his Milan Thriller Series, detailing his research process, character development, and the integration of Italian culture and history into his fast-paced, suspenseful narratives.

Master of International Thrillers

JACK ERICKSON

EXPLORING THE MILAN THRILLER SERIES AND THE INTRICACIES OF ITALIAN ANTI-TERRORISM

BY BEN ALAN

Jack Erickson is a master storyteller whose diverse literary portfolio spans international thrillers, mysteries, noir, true crime, and romantic suspense. His current passion project, the Milan Thriller Series, showcases Italy's anti-terrorism police, DIGOS, in a riveting sequence of novels. Beginning with "Thirteen Days in Milan," Erickson's journey through this series has captivated readers, leading to the release of "No One Sleeps" in 2017, "Vesuvius Nights" in 2019, and "The Lonely Assassin" in 2022.

Drawing inspiration from acclaimed mystery series such as Donna Leon's Commissario Brunetti, Andrea Camilleri's Inspector Montalbano, and Michael Dibdin's Aurelio Zen, Erickson infuses his work with the same rich textures of Italian culture and intricate plotting. His meticulous research, facilitated by connections with high-ranking officials at Milan's Questura, ensures authenticity in his depiction of the anti-terrorism landscape.

Erickson's deep ties to Italy, fostered through annual visits and intensive study at La Scuola da Vinci, imbue his narratives with a genuine Italian ambiance. His extensive background as an Air Force intelligence officer and a U.S. Senate speechwriter further enhances his ability to craft compelling, intricate stories that resonate with readers on multiple levels.

In this interview for Reader's House Magazine, Erickson delves into the inspirations behind his Milan Thriller Series, shares insights into his rigorous research process, and reflects on the creation of his resilient protagonist, Sylvia de Matteo. He also discusses the balancing act of weaving Italian history and culture into the fast-paced thrill of his novels and the impact of his previous careers on his writing style. Erickson's reflections offer a fascinating glimpse into the mind of a writer who seamlessly blends real-world experience with literary creativity.

What initially drew you to the setting of Milan and the world of anti-terrorism for your thriller series?

My wife and I retired in 2011 and traveled for a year. When we were in Italy, we spent two weeks in Menaggio on Lake Como. We took a train to Stazione Central train station in Milano on our way to Paris. While in

> Erickson's expert blend of intricate plots and authentic Italian settings cements his status as a distinguished author of international thrillers.

Stazione Centrale, I had 'un lumpo di genio,'a lightening bolt idea for the book that became my first Milan Thriller, "Thirteen Days in Milan." I spent the summer researching the plot, reading several books about contemporary Italy. I hired a researcher in Milano and gave her the basic plot. When I arrived in Milano, my researcher had arranged a meeting with the capo and chief deputy of Digos, the Italian anti-terrorism police at the Milano Questura (police headquarters).

Can you share insights into your research process for crafting authentic and intricate plots involving international terrorism and political intrigue?

Digos agents at Milano's Questura have provided me with valuable information about surveillance and tracking suspects for all four Milan Thrillers. I have traveled to Italia every year — except 2020, of course — and am fortunate to have Italian and American friends in Milano. Three of my Italian friends have been researchers for my Milan Thrillers. We have become close friends and I have met their families and enjoyed many meals with them. My researchers give me important information about my Italian characters, their careers, families, and lifestyle.

Your protagonist, Sylvia de Matteo, undergoes intense trials throughout the series. How do you approach developing her character and ensuring her resilience

resonates with readers?

In numerous conversations with my researchers and friends in Milano, I asked them for ideas on how a successful single mother, Sylvia de Matteo, would react if kidnapped and held as a prisoner for several weeks. My researchers and friends shared stories they had read or people they have known who find themselves in dangerous, life threatening situations.

The Milan Thriller Series explores various aspects of Italian society and culture. How do you balance incorporating these elements with maintaining the pacing and suspense of the story?

All of the Milan Thrillers have a connection to history. The prologue of "Thirteen Days in Milan" includes the gripping drama of the kidnapping and assassination in 1978 of five times Italian Prime Minister Aldo Moro by the left-wing terrorists Brigate Rosse (Red Brigades) who committed many violent crimes in the 1970's and 1980's. The terrorists who kidnap Sylvia de Matteo have a link to Brigate Rosse. By combining history with contemporary Italian political and social issues and conversations with Italian friends and researchers, I am able to write fiction with all the knowledge I have learned over the years. Reviews for all the Milan Thrillers have comments that they read as if written by an Italian.

Your novels have been compared to works by established authors such as Donna Leon and Andrea Camilleri. How do you feel about these comparisons, and do you draw inspiration from specific authors or genres?

I had read some of Donna Leon's and Andrea Camilleri's mysteries which take place in Venice (Donna Leon) and Sicily (Andrea Camilleri). After I started the Milan Thriller Series, I felt that my thrillers could become very popular because they took place in Milano, one of the most dynamic and historic cities in Europe, the center of finance, media, fashion, and art.

As a former intelligence officer and speechwriter, how have your past experiences influenced your approach to crafting intricate narratives and engaging dialogue in your novels?

My careers as an Air Force Intelligence Officer and later a speechwriter for three American Senators taught me how to research, interview important people, and reporting / writing a document that would be read by many. I have been a writer for more than 50 years and had two careers in publishing, writing five books on the early days of microbreweries and later writing international thrillers, short mysteries, true crime.

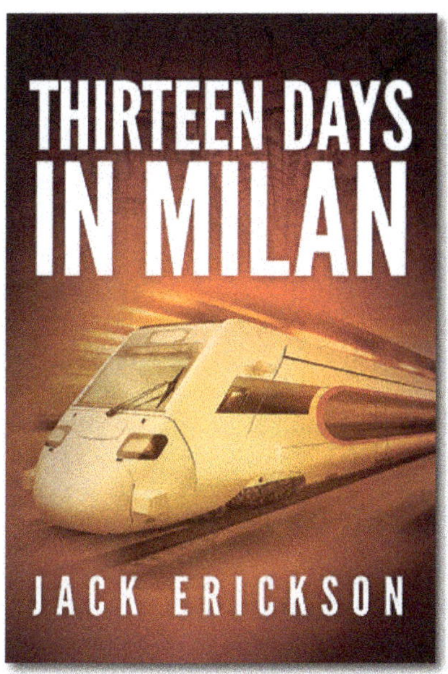

Thirteen Days in Milan is a riveting international thriller, blending intricate plots, vivid settings, and compelling characters seamlessly.

In Jack Erickson's *Thirteen Days in Milan*, readers are plunged into a gripping tale of international terrorism, political intrigue, and personal resilience. Set against the backdrop of Milan's bustling streets and the serene landscapes of the Italian Alps, the story follows Sylvia de Matteo, an American mother caught in the clutches of terrorists after a harrowing ordeal at Stazione Centrale.

Erickson's narrative unfolds with relentless tension, as Sylvia's plight becomes a high-stakes race against time for both the authorities and her captors. Through meticulously researched details and a keen eye for the complexities of Italian society, Erickson immerses readers in a world where alliances are fragile, and danger lurks at every turn.

Drawing inspiration from iconic mystery series like Donna Leon's Commissario Brunetti novels, Erickson crafts a narrative that is both thrilling and thought-provoking. As Milan's elite anti-terrorism unit, DIGOS, closes in on the perpetrators, the story delves into the intersections of politics, crime, and personal vendettas, offering a nuanced exploration of power and corruption.

At its core, *Thirteen Days in Milan* is a testament to the resilience of the human spirit in the face of adversity. Through Sylvia's journey, Erickson navigates themes of courage, sacrifice, and the enduring bonds of family. With its fast-paced plot, vivid imagery, and compelling characters, this novel is sure to captivate fans of international thrillers and leave them eagerly anticipating the next instalment in the Milan Thriller Series.

Dr. Cristina LePort, bestselling author and esteemed cardiologist, seamlessly blends her medical expertise with thrilling storytelling.

The Thrilling World of
CRISTINA LEPORT
ADVICE FOR ASPIRING AUTHORS

AS TOLD TO BEN ALAN

Dr. Cristina LePort is a name that resonates with both the medical and literary worlds. An Amazon Charts bestselling author, she has captivated readers with her gripping medical thrillers, blending her extensive expertise in cardiology and internal medicine with a flair for suspenseful storytelling. Her novel "DISSECTION" has garnered high praise from literary giants like Lee Child and Tess Gerritsen, and has achieved remarkable success across various international Amazon Kindle stores.

Born in Bologna, Italy, Dr. LePort graduated Summa cum Laude from the University of Bologna and is board certified in Internal Medicine, Cardiovascular Diseases, and Nuclear Cardiology. She currently serves as the Chief Medical Officer and co-founder of Genescient, a biotech company dedicated to genetic research on aging and longevity. Now residing in California with her husband, Dr. LePort continues to weave her medical knowledge into thrilling narratives that keep readers on the edge of their seats.

In this exclusive interview with Reader's House Magazine, Dr. LePort shares insights into her writing process, the inspiration behind her novels, and the seamless integration of her medical background into her fiction. From the heart-pounding emergencies in "DISSECTION" to the ethical dilemmas in "A Change of Heart," Dr. LePort's stories are a testament to her ability to balance scientific accuracy with compelling storytelling. Join us as we delve into the mind of a physician-turned-author who has mastered the art of medical thrillers.

The suspense comes from dealing with the medical world, bursting with life or death emergencies and the pressure of time. The technical details have to be minimized, so the reader doesn't get distracted.

> Dr. LePort masterfully combines medical precision with gripping suspense, creating unforgettable thrillers that captivate and educate readers.

The inspiration came from a TV commercial about aspirin. A man opened a card stating: "Your heart attack will arrive tomorrow"

I changed it to: "Your heart attack will arrive within one hour!" That's how DISSECTION started.

Although relatively infrequent in a cardiologist's daily practice, due to the often catastrophic nature, dissections are often unforgettable. I still remember arranging for emergency transport and following the ambulance in my car like in an action movie, after diagnosing a patient with a massively dilated and dissected aorta, hanging by a thread and ready to burst.

The scientific details have to be thoroughly integrated with the story and limited to what is necessary to

the story. Nothing kills suspense like an abstruse statement about a complicated medical procedure. We want the reader at the edge of his seat, not consulting a dictionary.

I wanted to write a novel with the background of heart transplant. I hope the readers appreciate the high stakes of the decisions and the many ethical issues involved.

I love to introduce futuristic elements in my stories. The technology I describe is often already possible, even if not fully realized. We live in wonderful times. Some of the things I described in my past books are already happening today, even before my books' publication dates.

Know what you write about. Write about a world you want to be in and any character you want to meet. The book about my present specialty, cardiology, was the first that I got published. I had great fun writing it.

Edit, correct and polish. I got many requests for a full manuscript after editing a version that had received only rejections.

Get help. Not by friend or family, but from dispassionate experts. I worked with several editors learning from each.

Don't give up. DISSECTION was rejected hundreds of times.

Keep on writing. I wrote 4 more books, while trying to publish my first one.

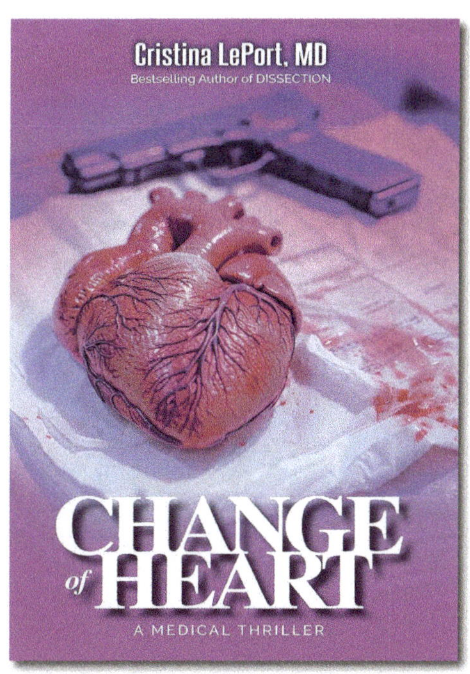

"Once again, Cristina LePort pens an excellent thriller, enlivened with vivid medical details and startling twists. She gets better with every novel!"
-Tess Gerritsen, New York Times Bestselling Author of the Spy Coasts

"Change if Heart is a dark and twisted medical thriller that moves at breakneck speed and will keep you up well past midnight."
-DP Lyle, Award-Winning Author, Co-Creator of the Outliers Writing University

EDITOR'S NOTE

Change of Heart by Dr. Cristina LePort is a gripping medical thriller that masterfully combines intricate medical details with relentless suspense. The well-developed characters and fast-paced plot make it impossible to put down. A must-read for fans of both medical dramas and crime thrillers.

P.C. James, acclaimed author of the Miss Riddell Cozy Mysteries, photographed near his home in Toronto, Canada.

Master of Cozy Mysteries

P.C. JAMES

CRAFTING CHARACTERS WITH COMPASSION AND HUMOUR

AS TOLD TO BEN ALAN

P.C. James, a master of the cozy mystery genre, has captivated readers with his charming and intricately plotted series, including the Miss Riddell Cozy Mysteries, the One Man and His Dog Cozy Mysteries, and the Royal Duchess and Sassy Senior Sleuths cozy mysteries, co-authored with Kathryn Mykel. Residing near Toronto, Canada, James balances his passion for wildlife photography with his dedication to crafting engaging narratives, often drawing inspiration from his own experiences and memories.

In this exclusive interview for Reader's House Magazine, James delves into the inspirations behind his beloved characters and series, the meticulous research that brings historical settings to life, and the delicate art of weaving humour into suspenseful plots. He also shares insights into his collaborative writing process and the personal anecdotes that enrich his storytelling. Join us as we explore the mind of P.C. James, a writer whose love for both the natural world and the written word continues to enchant and entertain readers around the globe.

You have created several beloved series, including the Miss Riddell Cozy Mysteries and One Man and His Dog Cozy Mysteries. What inspired you to write cozy mysteries, and how do you differentiate between the series in terms of tone and storytelling?

As a child and young man, I began reading my aunts' Christie, Sayer, and Heyer mysteries during wet summer holidays at their house in Ravenscar facing the North Sea.

Northern English weather being what it is, I had ample time for reading their books.

The defining moment, however, came with Joan Hickson playing Miss Marple. Because we'd moved to Canada in 1979, I didn't see Joan's interpretation until well into the 21st Century, long after my aunts were gone. Joan Hickson was so like my aunts, watching her Miss Marple was like being back at Ravenscar in the Fifties and Sixties and, along with the memories of my aunts and their mystery books, it made Miss Riddell's stories spring almost naturally from the page.

Your protagonist in the One Man and His Dog series, Tom Ramsay, is a retired inspector with a loyal border collie. What drew you to create a character who has retired from law enforcement, and how does Ramsay's background influence his approach to solving mysteries?

Inspector Ramsay in my Miss Riddell series was modeled on the men in my family when I was growing up. They were steady, serious people not given to emotional outbursts, whatever happened.

Ramsay had been a bit too unorthodox for his day, which didn't endear him to his superiors. I often had that feeling of 'differentness' during my career. What his personal history and unusual character bring to his investigations is compassion and an ability to see the many sides of people, without being overly judgemental.

And now I know how it feels to be retired so, again, it felt natural for me to write some stories with him as the central character.

Historical settings play a significant role in your books, such as England in the 1950s and 1960s. What research do you conduct to ensure the accuracy of these periods, and how do you weave historical details into your stories to enhance the narrative?

It's said older people can remember the distant past better than the near past and that's very true for me. I remember clearly events from my childhood and teenage years so setting the books in those years gives me an advantage over a younger author. That said, I do check my recollections to ensure I have them at the right time and place.

I also research songs and movies of the time because we lived out in the country then and didn't have much exposure to cultural events. No television or cinema in those days, for my family anyway.

In your new series co-authored with Kathryn Mykel, The Duchess of Snodsbury Amateur Detective Series, you introduce a duchess as a sleuth. What challenges and opportunities does this aristocratic setting provide for creating engaging mysteries and character dynamics?

Kathryn and I were in an online writing group together when we decided to co-author a cozy mystery series. Kathryn writes quilting craft-based cozy mysteries, and we thought a cozy mystery set in England in the Fifties when crafts were still everyday skills would be fun to do. I have a background and an understanding of how people behaved in the social structure of the time. These two different approaches make for difficult plotting sometimes, but the stories are well-received so we get there in the end.

Humour is a notable element in your Miss Riddell Cozy Mysteries. How do you balance humor with the suspense and intrigue of a mystery plot, and what role does humour play in developing your characters and their relationships?

To answer this, I'm going to shift inspiring authors from mysteries to my other favourite author, Jane Austen. I love the way Jane wrote her stories. There's humour in almost every sentence. I try to emulate her style because it keeps me reading and I hope it does the same for readers of my books.

As an author who loves photographing wildlife but spends much of your time writing, how do these two passions influence each other? Have your experiences with nature photography provided inspiration for any scenes or characters in your

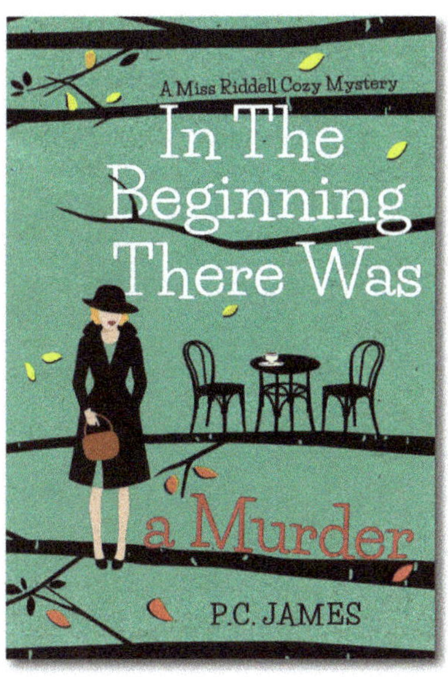

books?

The best example of my love of wildlife photography appearing in a book, is when Miss Riddell takes a cruise with her sister around the Galapagos Islands. Our own Galapagos cruise was a retirement present we gave ourselves, and we loved every minute of it. One scene in Murder on a Galapagos Cruise is of a fellow cruise guest, upon landing on another island and being told how we'd see even more iguanas, groaning, 'not another '@'!' iguana.' I liked that so much, I put it in my story. I also used my wildlife photography experience in the two books set in Australia.

Championing Truth Through Fiction

JEFF KELLAND

Addressing Inequality and Environmental Crisis Through Art

BY BEN ALAN

Jeff R. Kelland, a 65-year-old Canadian author, embodies a profound concern for societal welfare and a fervent passion for the written word. With an extensive background that includes innumerable essays, magazine articles, editorials, poetry, and prose, Jeff has made a significant mark in various publications. His academic achievements, which include a first-class honours B.A. in philosophy and German, a Master of Science in Community Health from Memorial University's School of Medicine, and a ground-breaking thesis, further underscore his intellectual rigor. Beyond his written work, Jeff is a sought-after public speaker for numerous national and provincial causes and conferences, a visual artist, and a veteran singer-songwriter and entertainer with over 40 years of experience.

In this interview, Jeff delves into the inspirations and motivations behind his novel The Dying Party, which addresses the urgent themes of climate change and societal collapse. Following the publication of Grace Ungiven, Jeff turned his focus to the increasingly pressing issue of climate change, driven by the realization that humanity is failing to meet climate goals and is, in fact, losing ground. His extensive research, spanning over a year, revealed the alarming truth that time is running out, compelling him to write The Dying Party and its prequel novella Two of All People.

Jeff shares insights into his meticulous research process, ensuring that the scenarios in his novel are both scientifically plausible and emotionally impactful. He discusses how his personal concerns and empathy for those already suffering in equatorial regions influenced his writing. Furthermore, Jeff emphasizes the crucial role of fiction in raising awareness about climate change and motivating readers to take action. He candidly discusses the challenges of depicting the stark disparity between the rich and the poor through alternating storylines that offer a realistic portrayal of the crisis.

In exploring the psychological impact of climate change on humanity, Jeff reflects on the future for our children and grandchildren, dedicating his work

Jeff R. Kelland discusses his novel The Dying Party, addressing climate change, societal collapse, and the disparity between rich and poor, driven by extensive research and a passion for impactful storytelling.

Jeff Kelland's "The Dying Party" is a masterfully crafted, gripping exploration of humanity's response to climate catastrophe. Through dual narratives of survival and escape, Kelland delivers a poignant, thought-provoking warning about the future. This compelling, research-driven novel is a must-read for those concerned about our planet's fate.

Jeff Kelland masterfully intertwines narrative craft with social activism, creating compelling stories that illuminate profound truths and inspire change.

to his own grandchildren. After poignantly addressing the Catholic clerical child sexual abuse crisis in his first book Grace Ungiven, and then tackling the climate change crisis with The Dying Party, he points to the lack of progress. Jeff's realization of humanity's failure to protect its own children has profoundly changed him, and he hopes that The Dying Party will serve as a catalyst for greater awareness and action.

What inspired you to write The Dying Party and explore the themes of climate change and societal collapse in such a detailed and personal way?

After writing and publishing "Grace Ungiven", I thought there could scarcely be a topic that needed a light shone on it as much as the Catholic clerical child sexual abuse and child sexual abuse in general. But coming to realize that we aren't meeting our climate change goals, and that we are in fact losing ground, I decided to do some research on the matter. This stretched into more than a year, and it wasn't long before I realized that we are running out of time. There could be nothing more serious than the loss of all of humanity, so I decided to write "The Dying Party" and its sequel novella "Two of All People".

Can you share some insights into the research process for the novel? How did you ensure that the scenarios depicted were both scientifically plausible and emotionally impactful?

The research involved discovering that we have made no progress whatsoever on benchmarks set by the Kyoto Protocol and the other efforts to reach consensus and spur action. It also looked at the early results of the newest research into the many ominous changes taking place in the world and humanity as we move ever closer to disaster. I must admit that my own concerns became a factor, which allowed me to empathize with people already suffering in equatorial regions, and prognosticate about future scenarios as the situation worsens.

How do you envision the role of fiction in raising awareness about climate change and motivating action among readers? What impact do you hope The Dying Party will have on its audience?

As a writer, I have to believe that the arts are and always have been our best means to consider and understand issues, to generate solutions to what faces us at any given time, or to at the very last raise awareness. While I needed to be realistic about the kind of impact one book can make, I felt the seriousness of the matter demanded a depiction of "the worst that could happen". It was dirty job, as they say, and it is not what people want to think about (which is the problem) but somebody had to do it.

How do you balance the portrayal of the stark disparity between the rich and the poor with the personal stories of your characters?

Given that my research shows that one of the factors causing climate change and keeping us from effective, pro-active solutions is the ever-widening gap between the rich and the poor, I decided to portray this with two separate alternating story lines – one about the plight and limited options of a handful of the less fortunate who have no choice but to accept their fate, and one about some people among the rich and powerful who will not accept it and are trying to save themselves somehow. This made for a more realistic story while providing valuable insights into the full range of possible scenarios the crisis holds for human beings.

What research or real-world events influenced the development of the novel's depiction of a future ravaged by climate change, and what inspired you to explore the psychological impact of climate change on humanity in Two of All People and The Dying Party"?

It was not research or any real-world event that influenced me to depict a future ravaged by climate change, nor to explore the psychological impact of climate change on humanity. The birth of the project and the impetus for research came about when considering the future for our children and grandchildren, and the book is dedicated to my own grandchildren. Most troubling of all, however, is that the subject of my first novel *Grace Ungiven* as well as the subject of "The Dying Party", and the lack of any progress being made on either of the crises they address, show us that we are in effect abandoning our own children – abandoning Catholic children to the wicked wiles of the Catholic church's patriarchy on the one hand, and abandoning all our children and grandchildren to a short and horrific future on a deteriorating planet. I would never have thought it of us, and the realization that this is what we are doing has changed me

Sandy Rosenthal, founder of
Levees.org and author of 'Words
Whispered in Water', at her home
in New Orleans.

Strategies for Change

SANDY ROSENTHAL

EFFECTIVE ACTIVISM IN THE FACE OF ADVERSITY

AS TOLD TO ANNA HARLOWE

Amid the devastation of Hurricane Katrina and the subsequent levee failures in New Orleans, one woman's determination to uncover the truth sparked a movement that would change the course of disaster accountability. Sandy Rosenthal, founder of the non-profit Levees.org, has become a beacon of resilience and advocacy, challenging powerful institutions and demanding transparency. Her book, *Words Whispered in Water*, details her relentless pursuit to expose the Army Corps of Engineers' role in the catastrophe and their attempts to conceal their mistakes.

In this compelling interview, Rosenthal shares her journey from suspicion to revelation, the challenges she faced in establishing Levees.org, and the strategies that proved effective in her fight for justice. She also reflects on the personal impact of her work, the accolades she has received, and the importance of maintaining balance through her diverse interests. Join us as we delve into the story of a woman who turned tragedy into a crusade for truth and accountability, inspiring countless others to stand up for their communities.

Words Whispered in Water details your journey to uncover the truth behind the flooding in New Orleans during Hurricane Katrina. What initially sparked your suspicion about the official explanations, and how did you begin your investigation into the real cause of the levee failures?

My suspicion was sparked when I read official testimony provided at one of the very first Katrina congressional hearings which corroborated my own theory. And so my investigation began to find the true culprit in the breach catastrophe. I started by asking hard questions. When I was harassed and/or ridiculed for asking these questions, I perceived that as further evidence that my theory was accurate.

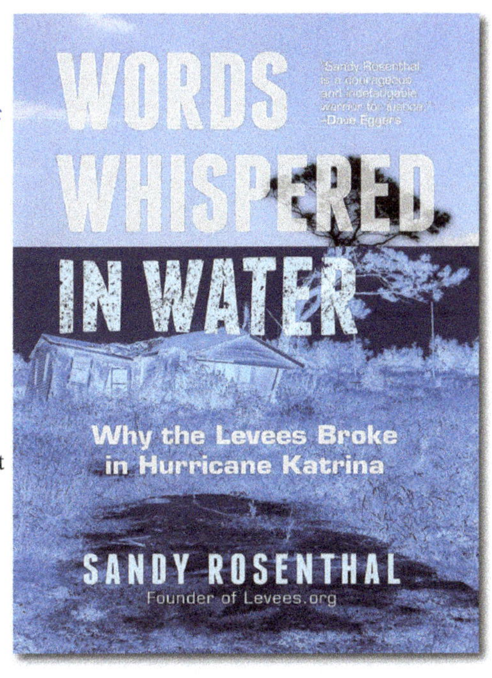

Founding Levees.org during the chaos of the 2005 storm was a remarkable feat. What were some of the biggest challenges you faced in establishing and growing this nonprofit, and how did you overcome them to garner 25,000 supporters and chapters in five states?

A bothersome challenge was the hundreds of vicious anonymous comments targeting me and my fifteen year old son that lasted for several years. These comments appeared publicly online associated with stories in the local newspaper. I prevailed by viewing the abusive comments as free advice. Information is often lurking in the words of people with a hidden agenda, especially when they speak in shrill tones.

We achieved the membership of 25K when we wrote federal legislation and we got U.S. Senator Mary Landrieu to sponsor it. The bill called for the 8/29 Investigation which would be a truly independent federal investigation of the catastrophe. While we didn't succeed in obtaining the investigation, but we did sigificantly grow the membership.

The numerous state chapters were made possible by the fact that two thirds of our supporter base lived outside of Louisiana. To this day, this base remains highly engaged in the work of Levees.org

Your efforts have earned you numerous accolades, including Outstanding Social Entrepreneur of the Year from Tulane University and Most Influential Woman from Mount Holyoke College. How have these recognitions impacted your work and advocacy, and what do they mean to you personally?

The awards have impacted my work in two ways. They are proof to my current base of supporters that their help is generating results and a sign that their time has been well invested. They have also been a way to garner even more support because media attention to the awards helps further the reach of my organization's message. As for what they mean to me personally, they mean little. They would not have happened without the Levees.org supporters.

In your book, you emphasize the importance of exposing bad behavior by large organizations and bureaucracies. What strategies did you find most effective in compelling the news media and the government to acknowledge the true cause of the flooding, and what advice would you give to other citizen activists facing similar challenges?

I found the number one tool for government compliance was the Public Record Request (PRR) for state government and requests under the Freedom of Information Act (FOIA) or the federal government. I feel that these tools are underutlized. And I have also found that responses to PRRs and FOIAs tend to provide additional surprising and important information previously not widely known.

My advice to citizen activists looking to get their mission in the media is to 1) ask a reasonable question 2) make a valid point and 3) back it up with data. That's how you get the attention of the media when large organizations commit bad behavior.

As a resident of New Orleans, how has your personal connection to the city influenced your activism and your determination to uncover the truth? How

has your relationship with the city evolved since Hurricane Katrina?

If I ever questioned my decision and my passion to find the truth, all I had to do was look around me for reminders. I was surrounded on all sides by people who had suffered losses. They may have lost personal belongings, their entire home, their community, their job and maybe a loved one. I am closer to the people of New Orleans because we experienced and survived a catastrophe.

Beyond your activism, you have a diverse range of interests, from playing tennis and practicing yoga to dancing to zydeco music. How do these activities contribute to your overall well-being and balance, especially given the demanding nature of your advocacy work?

Hardly a day has passed since Aug 29, 2005 when I have not done some sort of exercise. It might be a game of tennis, practicing yoga or maybe going to a local dance hall for zydeco music. At a bare minimum, I would take my two dogs for a long walk. I believe physical exercise keeps the mind healthy and prevents burnout. I have also found that exercise seems to make big problems get smaller. They don't go away completely, but they become solvable.

> Sandy Rosenthal's relentless pursuit of truth and justice has profoundly impacted disaster accountability and inspired countless citizen activists.

Exploring the Georgian Era with Lucinda Brant

LUCINDA BRANT

Unveiling the Secrets of the 18th Century Through Engaging Narratives and Authentic Characters

BY DAN PETERS

Lucinda Brant discusses her passion for the Georgian era, commitment to historical accuracy, and the development of her richly detailed, immersive historical romances.

Reader's House Magazine is delighted to feature an exclusive interview with Lucinda Brant, a distinguished author whose captivating Georgian-era historical romances and mysteries have earned her bestseller status on the New York Times, USA Today, Amazon, and Audible. With her works translated into multiple languages and available in audio, eBook, and print, Brant has enchanted readers worldwide with her meticulous attention to historical detail and rich storytelling.

Lucinda Brant's journey into historical fiction is deeply rooted in her academic achievements and personal passion for the 18th century. Her extensive education, including a Bachelor of Arts degree and a Post Graduate Diploma in Education, has profoundly influenced her writing. She credits her university experience with developing the critical thinking skills necessary for rigorous historical research and her teaching career with honing her ability to present history engagingly.

The 18th century, particularly the Georgian era, continues to inspire Brant's work. She is drawn to the era's fascinating contradictions, where a society valuing order and restraint also embraced boisterousness and a zest for life. This duality is vividly reflected in her characters, providing readers with an authentic glimpse into the complexities of the time.

Brant's novels often explore the lives of the aristocracy, a choice driven by her fascination with the period's social structures and the symbolic significance of fashion and manners. She strives to dispel common misconceptions about Georgian aristocrats, portraying them as complex individuals deeply concerned with their world and future.

Historical accuracy is a cornerstone of Brant's writing. Her extensive research process ensures that her stories are grounded in the realities of the past, seamlessly blending historical authenticity with compelling narratives. Her commitment to maintaining historical integrity without compromising the entertainment value of her stories sets her work apart.

The Roxton Foundation Series, a fan-favorite, delves into themes of love, scandal, and societal expectations in 18th-century England and France. Inspired by her readers' curiosity about the characters' lives beyond the original stories, Brant expands on their adventures and challenges, enriching her richly

The captivating works of Lucinda Brant, known for their historical accuracy and immersive storytelling, beloved by readers worldwide.

woven tapestry of historical fiction.

Lucinda Brant's ability to create immersive and emotionally resonant stories has captivated readers across cultures and eras. Her well-developed characters and engaging narratives transcend time, connecting with the universal human experiences of joy, loss, hope, and love. Join us as we explore the mind and works of this remarkable author in our insightful interview.

Your background includes a rich mix of academic achievements, from a Bachelor of Arts degree to a Post Graduate Diploma in Education. How have these qualifications shaped your approach to historical fiction writing?

From the age of 11 I've been collecting and adding to my library that focuses on all aspects of the Eighteenth Century, but university provided me with the critical thinking skills needed to bring academic rigor to my historical fiction writing. While teaching high school students provided the perfect platform to present history in an engaging way.

You've expressed a deep passion for the 18th century, particularly the Georgian era. What aspects of this period continue to inspire and captivate you, both in your writing and personal interests?

I'm fascinated by the contradictions of the Eighteenth Century. On the one hand, Georgians expected life to be ordered, they valued politeness and manners, practiced restraint, and strove to live in comfort. Yet, they were also boisterous,

forthright, often resorted to violence, were greedy and gluttonous, and had a zest for life. I hope that the experiences of my characters reflect these contradictions and provide my readers with an insight into such a fascinating era.

In many ways the Georgian era mirrors our own. They asked questions about their place in the world. They went exploring across vast unchartered oceans, while we have gone beyond our planet to explore the vastness of space. There were many medical, scientific, and technological breakthroughs during the 1700s that made life more bearable, livable, and safer: inoculation against smallpox, the discovery of anesthesia and electricity, the wearing of Bifocals, the use of lightning rods for the first time, furniture created solely for comfort, to name a few. And this will surprise most, by the mid-1700s Parisians were installing indoor flushable toilets. The Georgian era was also a time when people gave themselves permission to enjoy life for its own sake. Such a novel concept went out of vogue with the Victorians and didn't resurface again until the early 20th Century after World War One, during the 1920s.

In your novels, you focus on aristocratic characters living in the Georgian era. What draws you to this social stratum, and how do you strive to present a nuanced portrayal of aristocratic life beyond stereotypes?

Writing about the aristocracy gives me greater scope to showcase what it is I love and find fascinating about the 1700s. Clothing was vitally important to the Georgians. What you wore told the world what you were—aristocrat, tradesperson, servant, pauper. And the spectacle of fashionable clothing for the eighteenth-century aristocratic male was not so unfamiliar to me, who grew up in the 1970s—also a time when men were able to outwardly express their inner pe-

acock, in tight satin suits in vibrant colors, platform shoes, and bouffant hair.

I also hope to dispel the myths that became entrenched in the Victorian era that their noble Georgian grandparents were unwashed, immoral, corrupt care-for-nobodies. The Georgians cared very much about the world they lived in. They worried about the future for their children. Most had companionate marriages and set out to live productive lives. They were farmers, politicians, diplomats, bureaucrats, soldiers, scientists, writers, philosophers and patrons of the arts, sciences, and exploration. And just as we are obsessed with billionaire and celebrity lives today, so, too, the Georgians were obsessed with the lives of their first families.

Your commitment to historical accuracy is evident in your writing. Can you tell us more about your research process and how you balance historical authenticity with storytelling?

Of course, story is everything; entertaining the reader is paramount. I try to use my research to ground the characters in time and place without overwhelming the reader in a history lesson. We've all seen the iceberg meme, with the tip just showing above the waterline, which is the historical research used in a book, and the vast size of the iceberg hidden in the depths, showing all the research that was done but never used. Yet no research is ever wasted, I just set it aside to be used in future books. And I won't compromise historical accuracy for the sake of the story. Without that, historical fiction is mere costume fantasy.

Your Roxton Foundation Series explores themes of love, scandal, and societal expectations in 18th-century England and France. What inspired you to create this series, and what messages or insights do you

hope readers will take away from it?

This series is for the fans of Noble Satyr—the Duke of Roxton and Antonia Moran's rocky road to a happily ever after—who kept asking me what happened after the couple married, and the intervening 24 years before their son and heir's love story told in Midnight Marriage (the first book in the Roxton Family Saga series).

Noble Satyr is now also the first book in this new Foundation series, with books 2, 3 & 4 exploring the first years of the Duke and Antonia's marriage, with their newborn son, and how they navigate the social corridors of Versailles where nobles live surrounded by opulence yet are shackled by rigid protocol. Living beyond their means to keep up appearances, Roxton's French cousins are resentful of his wealth and influence and plot his societal downfall. Steadfast and deeply in love, the couple are up to any challenge!

Your books are known for their immersive storytelling and well-developed characters. How do you approach character development and crafting engaging narratives that resonate with readers across different cultures and time periods?

Fashion, politics, customs and manners, technologies, and ideas, all have changed and evolved over time, but human nature—the way we think, feel and act—is embedded in our psyche. So, while my characters inhabit an eighteenth-century world, and act accordingly to their time and place, it is their feelings of joy, loss, hope, pride, and most importantly how they love, that are universal and eternal. Which is why I think readers from around the globe and from all walks of life enjoy my stories.

Angel Giacomo, author and former law enforcement officer, draws on her rich experiences to craft authentic and engaging military thrillers.

Mastering the Art of Mystery

ANGEL GIACOMO

JOURNEY INTO MILITARY THRILLERS

AS TOLD TO DAN PETERS

Angel Giacomo's "The Jackson MacKenzie Chronicles" series offers readers thrilling narratives infused with realism, honoring the sacrifices of military heroes.

Angel Giacomo is a multifaceted individual whose journey from law enforcement to writing is as compelling as the stories she crafts. With a background as a field officer, explosives detection K-9 handler, and fatality traffic investigator, Angel has a wealth of experiences that inform her writing. Her academic pursuits in Political Science and History, combined with her dedication to supporting veterans, particularly those from the Vietnam War era, add layers of authenticity and depth to her work. Her debut novel, "The Jackson MacKenzie Chronicles: In the Eye of the Storm," published in 2020, is a testament to her ability to weave intricate narratives that resonate with readers seeking both excitement and realism.

Angel's life is a tapestry of diverse experiences, from handling explosives and attending FEMA classes to playing the trombone and washing dishes. These varied roles have enriched her storytelling, allowing her to create characters and plots that are both believable and engaging. Her commitment to meticulous research ensures that her action scenes and technical details are accurate, providing readers with an immersive experience.

In this interview, Angel Giacomo shares insights into her transition from law enforcement to writing, the influences behind her characters and plots, and her dedication to exploring the psychological and emotional struggles of veterans. She also discusses her family cookbook, "Giacomo Family Recipes," which reflects her love for cooking and her desire to share her family's culinary traditions. Join us as we delve into the mind of a writer who brings authenticity and passion to every page.

After a successful and varied career in law enforcement and other fields, what inspired you to transition into writing, particularly military thrillers?

I have been writing most of my life, including high school and college papers, but not fiction. Writing was a part of my police career. Report writing is stating the facts, nothing more. I started writing fiction in my 20s to unwind after work. I am an avid history reader. My father served in the US Navy from 1959-1970 and the Army National Guard from 1976-1992, so I gravitated to writing military fiction. Having spent years on the front lines, witnessing firsthand the complexi-

<blockquote>Angel Giacomo masterfully blends authenticity and passion, creating compelling narratives that honor veterans and captivate readers with realism and depth.</blockquote>

ties and high-stakes nature of law enforcement, I felt compelled to bring these realities to life through fiction. I aim to provide an authentic glimpse into the emotional challenges faced by those in the military. My background allows me to infuse my stories with realism and depth, creating compelling narratives that resonate with readers seeking excitement and authenticity.

Your debut novel, The Jackson MacKenzie Chronicles: In the Eye of the Storm, draws from your extensive experience with law enforcement and military knowledge. How did your background influence the development of your characters and plot?

My background had a significant influence on my characters and plot. Jackson was based on several people, including one by happy accident, as I didn't learn how much a friend's journey to West Point was nearly identical to Jackson's until after In the Eye of the Storm was published. The first person to enter Jackson's development was Lt. General Hal Moore. Another would be Colonel James Nicholas "Nick" Rowe. Those two men went through the same kind of hell that I placed Jackson. Writing allowed me to contribute to the conversation about the sacrifices and heroism of those in uniform. It offers a platform to honor their service and explore the intricate dynamics of duty, honor, and camaraderie.

Your work spans multiple careers, from handling explosives to washing dishes at a restaurant. How do these diverse experiences shape the authenticity and depth of your storytelling?

My experiences significantly enhance the authenticity and depth of my storytelling. Each job provided unique insights into different aspects of life, contributing to the tapestry of experiences and feelings intertwined in my writing. That gives me the ability to write with realism.

I recently helped the reunion group for the 85th Evacuation Hospital with the book Anthology: Tales of the 85th Evacuation Hospital, Phu Bai. I edited their true stories of sacrifice and courage in the face of overwhelming odds to achieve a 95% survival rate. Their motto was Miracularum Laborantes," in Latin means "Miracle Workers." My service pales in comparison to theirs.

You have attended numerous FEMA classes and have handled various weapons. How do these experiences inform the action scenes and the technical accuracy in your books?

My lifetime of past experiences helped shape what is written in my books to go along with my meticulous research. I want to get the facts right. If I don't, I could be on the receiving end of a bad review.

The Jackson MacKenzie Chronicles explores the personal and professional impacts of

war. What motivated you to delve into the psychological and emotional struggles of veterans in your writing?

PTSD is not exclusive to the military. It happens in all walks of life, including the police department, crime victims, collision survivors, and victims of tragedy. It is an ongoing tragedy for the military as the government machine chews up the soldiers, sailors, airmen, and Marines and spits them out to their own devices. Twenty-two veterans a day commit suicide. That is a tragic statistic. Maybe writing a character or more with PTSD will shed light on the issue. I aim to provide an authentic glimpse into the emotional challenges faced by those in the military. My background allows me to infuse my stories with realism and depth, creating compelling narratives that resonate with readers seeking excitement and authenticity.

Aside from your novels, you've also written a family cookbook, Giacomo Family Recipes. How does this project reflect your personal history, and what inspired you to share your family's culinary traditions with your readers?

Simple. I love to cook. The recipes came from a family reunion. Copies of the actual written recipes are included in the book.

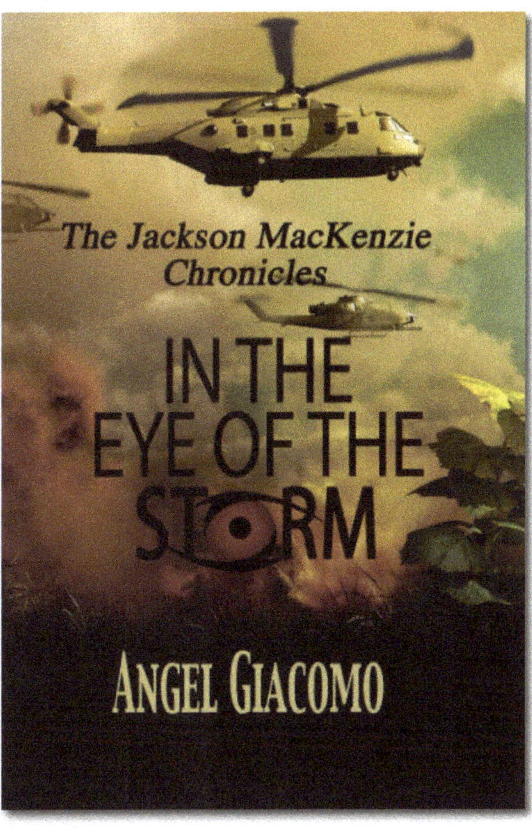

<blockquote>Angel Giacomo's "The Jackson MacKenzie Chronicles: In the Eye of the Storm" is a gripping masterpiece that delves into the harrowing realities of war. With vivid storytelling and profound character development, it captures the resilience and turmoil of Lt. Colonel Jackson MacKenzie. This award-winning novel is a poignant tribute to the sacrifices of soldiers, leaving readers deeply moved and reflective.</blockquote>

The Inspirational Journey of

JOSEPH FAGARAZZI

How Life's Journey Shapes Stories of Empathy and Resilience

BY BEN ALAN

Joseph Fagarazzi's life reads like an epic novel of endurance, triumph, and relentless self-discovery. Born in Venice, Italy, on September 7, 1951, his early years were marred by the harshness of an unloving and dismissive family. The late 1950s saw young Joseph placed in a convent as his parents moved to London. It wasn't until 1960, thanks to the intervention of his uncle, that Joseph was finally reunited with his parents in England. Despite facing a cruel and passive-aggressive father, Joseph's optimism never wavered. He believed that hardship could be a driving force, propelling one forward to survive and thrive.

In 1977, Joseph married his Australian wife, and by 1978, they had moved to Australia, where he began managing clothing stores. His entrepreneurial spirit flourished, leading to the ownership of three stores over 22 years. Not stopping there, Joseph ventured into property development, successfully selling units and retaining several as rentals. In 2006, he transitioned to real estate, achieving a Diploma of Property Services and a Certificate IV in Property Services.

Retiring in 2015, Joseph turned his focus back to his artistic roots and began writing. His memoir, *Escaping My Demons*, is a poignant reflection on his turbulent childhood and a testament to his belief in the power of resilience. Joseph's journey from a ridiculed child to a successful businessman and author is nothing short of inspirational. Through his story, he aims to provide hope and guidance to those with similar backgrounds, demonstrating that it is possible to overcome adversity and find peace.

In our interview, Joseph delves into the emotional depths of his

Joseph Fagarazzi's story highlights his journey from a ridiculed child in Venice to a successful businessman and author in Australia, showcasing resilience, creativity, and inner.

experiences, revealing what motivated him to share such a personal and painful story with the world. He discusses the cathartic process of writing *Escaping My Demons*, how it allowed him to confront his inner turmoil, and the sense of peace it ultimately brought him. Joseph also offers insights into his enduring optimism, sharing how he found the strength to persevere despite significant trauma and abuse. His advice to others facing similar hardships is both practical and deeply empathetic.

Our conversation also explores the pivotal moments and decisions that transformed his life, the importance of self-belief, and the power of persistence. Joseph reflects on his diverse career, from managing clothing stores to real estate, and how each phase shaped his perspective on life. He emphasizes the importance of igniting and sustaining one's inner drive, and the transformative impact of creative pursuits in processing the past.

Joseph Fagarazzi's story is a compelling testament to the resilience of the human spirit. His journey from an unwanted child in Venice to a successful businessman and inspiring author in Australia offers profound lessons in overcoming adversity, embracing creativity, and finding inner peace.

Escaping My Demons delves into the deep emotional and physical hardships you faced as a child. What motivated you to share such a personal and painful story with the world, and how did writing the book contribute to your healing process?

11 years ago I started writing a five-page letter to myself, it was to be a self-healing process. It helped "me" find a way to stop struggling with my inner emotional scars and a depressive state of mind, once I finished writing I then placed it in the freezer, It was a way to freeze the pain I was enduring at the time not realizing that 11 years later it became a stepping stone towards my memoir (Escaping My Demons).

As I was reaching the final stages of my book it dawned on me that jotting it down on paper gave me the inner peace I was longing for and realized that living with hate is not inspirational and finally understood that our time on this earth is ticking away and we should stop worrying about the past but instead we should be looking ahead to what makes us happy.

You experienced significant trauma and abuse from your father during your childhood. How did you find the resilience and strength to remain optimistic about your future, and what advice would you give to others facing similar circumstances?

The self-belief was the hardest thing to gain but eventually, I realized I was not the no-hoper my parents perceived me to be. I fought back my Demons, managed to survive, and succeeded in becoming a successful retired businessman by theoretically changing my ideologies and how I viewed things!

I started treating my life as a blueprint, it now defines the life I want.

The blueprint summarises the successes and failures we have and how we react to them.

Experiencing knockbacks, especially from my family throughout my life, caused me significant stress and for that, I constantly struggled with my self-worth. Opposing this belief was the hardest thing to do but I eventually realized that nothing changes unless you change it yourself.

Your journey from being an unwanted child in Venice to a successful businessman and property developer in Australia is remarkable. What were some of the key turning points or decisions that helped you transform your life despite your early hardships?

I learned to fight and work hard for what I wanted and I can proudly I never asked for free handouts because I always felt there would always be someone to remind me. I learned "Not" to change their characteristics because the burden/issues I carried were from within and I allowed my Demons to follow my every move.

They followed me in my darkest moments and not knowing what to do I hoisted the heavy pieces of baggage on my shoulders throughout my years.

At the time it didn't register that only "me" and only "me" alone could resolve these issues with only a vision of clarity.

After retiring in 2015, you returned to your passion for art and began writing your book. How have these creative pursuits helped you

Joseph Fagarazzi's 'Escaping My Demons' is an extraordinary memoir, adorned with multiple awards, detailing his harrowing childhood marked by neglect and abuse. His journey from despair to success is a testament to resilience and offers profound inspiration to all who have faced adversity."

process your past, and what role do they play in your life now?

My creative pursuits were monumental in achieving a life of happiness,

Writing my book although it made me relive the past, it also gave me inner peace to move on with my life.

My paintings were a form of rehabilitation or an intermission that kept my mind occupied by not thinking of the past.

In Escaping My Demons, you hope to help others with similar upbringings. What specific messages or lessons do you want readers to take away from your story, and how do you believe your experiences can inspire others?

I stopped making excuses by blaming the obstacles that were blocking my path to happiness.

The fundamental flow I had in my darkest days was to seemingly find excuses and blame something or someone for my misery, but I then realized that the latter would always be there and had to change my mindset.

I am hoping my story will inspire, have a positive impact and benefit those who faced and continue to face childhood trauma.

I would also hope that biased parents out there who purposely destroy their child's mental ability to grow and prosper consider learning from my parents' mistakes and start showing love and support not only to their wanted child but also to the unwanted ones that were born by mistake.

Your career has spanned various fields, including managing clothing stores, property development, and real estate. How did these diverse experiences shape your perspective on life, and what did you learn from each phase of your professional journey that you might share with aspiring entrepreneurs?

I had to ignite the fire in me and keep it burning to succeed!

My will and determination to survive have always been my strength and above all the love and support of a loving wife by my side.

Persistence is the key, keep following your dream and never give up!

I continued to believe that by keeping the fire burning within, you will then discover that the hardship bestowed on you will make you stronger and more determined than ever.

Don't let your ego take over your success and show a little respect and empathy to those worse off than you, cherish your achievements and if you can help others.

Consider my book to be a survival life-changing kit, it is written by someone who has experienced hardship and eventually found happiness by moving on.

PHOTO: Joseph Fagarazzi's incredible life story and powerful memoir inspire others to overcome adversity and embrace their own resilience and creativity.

Terry Lister, seasoned traveler and author, shares his global adventures and cultural insights with readers worldwide.

TERRY LISTER

TERRY'S QUEST FOR AUTHENTIC EXPERIENCES

AS TOLD TO DAN PETERS

Terry Lister's journey from a successful career in accounting and government to becoming a seasoned solo traveller and writer is nothing short of inspiring. With a background as a partner at Deloitte and a Minister in the Government of Bermuda, Terry's life took a transformative turn when he retired at 60 and embarked on a quest to explore the world. Since 2014, he has visited 103 countries, including 23 in Africa, immersing himself in diverse cultures and experiences. His travels have not only broadened his horizons but also deepened his understanding of the world, which he passionately shares through his writing.

In this exclusive interview with Reader's House Magazine, Terry delves into the motivations behind his travels and the profound impact they have had on his perspective. He discusses his books, "Immersed in West Africa" and "A New Day Dawns," which document his adventures across West African countries, shedding light on the region's rich cultural tapestry. Terry also shares insights from his book "Peace, Joy and Love: Christmas in Africa," offering a unique glimpse into how Christmas is celebrated across different African nations.

Terry's experiences as a solo traveller in less touristy regions like West Africa highlight the challenges and rewards of seeking authentic experiences. His travelogues aim to dispel stereotypes and emphasize the cultural richness and diversity of Africa. Drawing from his background in accounting and government, Terry offers valuable advice to aspiring travellers who wish to explore regions like West Africa independently. Join us as we explore the world through Terry Lister's eyes and discover the transformative power of travel.

Your transition from a partner at Deloitte and a Minister in the Bermuda government to a solo traveller and writer is quite a departure. What inspired you to embark on this new chapter of life, and how has it influenced your perspective on travel and exploration?

I was born a traveller. My father and two of his brothers were often 'away'. They simply had a yearning to see the world. So I acted as I saw. I knew they had a better understanding of the world because of their travels and I wanted the same. My family this is who we are.

In Bermuda male life expectancy is 74. Thus, I had no desire to work beyond 60.

For me there is the joy/anguish of being in places I only dreamed about. On Goree Island standing at the Door of No Return drew a feeling of numbness. I neither shouted nor cried. I was just numb.

I travel to 'see for myself' and thus my views and opinions have sometimes been changed by what I have seen but overall they are strengthened because of being there.

Your books Immersed in West Africa and A New Day Dawns document your solo travels across several West African countries. What motivated you to explore this region, and could you share a particularly memorable experience or encounter from your journeys?

East Africa, South Africa and North Africa are relatively well known outside of Africa. So I chose West Africa as it is not as well known. At that point I had not decided to write about my travels but given that I have, it's easier to shape readers curiosity by writing about places they may know little about.

I do extensive research before traveling and this determines where I go and what I see. I had learnt that slavery was still the norm in Mauritania. I was determined to see this for myself. I learnt that the border between Senegal and Mauritania has been regarded as the most corrupt border crossing in the world. That worried me a bit. So when I was goung to Mauritania from Senegal I was very aware of my surroundings. Upon arrival a policeman took me and others off the bus and to the police station. After waiting, I was ushered into a room where all

the formalities to stamp me out of Senegal where performed. Instead of crossing the river into Mauritania, the policeman took me into another building to a room full of men. He turned me over to the leader who asked me to show him all of my money. I refused. I was told I had to change my money then they offered me a really lousy rate. I refused again. So one of the others shouted, "You Have to change it with us. We are the black market."

Peace, Joy and Love: Christmas in Africa offers a unique perspective on how Christmas is celebrated across different African nations. What inspired you to write about this topic, and what are some of the most surprising or heart-warming traditions you encountered during your research?

As I travelled I was first surprised by the extent of Islam religion in West Africa. I wondered how the Christians and Muslims interacted especially at holiday time. I was happy to know that in most countries both religions were respected and there was little hostility.

Knowing Christmas to be the biggest religious festival on the Christian calendar, I decided to study how this played out. I was pleased, for example, to observer that while Senegal is 95% Muslim, the people in the cities fully embrace Christmas including buying Christmas trees and sharing Christmas meals. I was disappointed that the tiny number of Christians in countries such as Mauritania and Tunisia were almost criminalized for celebrating Christmas.

While there were many traditions observed many people followed the practice of having the family get together in the village. In Sierra Leone many people return from their homes overseas to be with family at this time.

As a traveler who values authentic experiences, how do you balance the challenges and rewards of solo travel, especially in less touristy regions like West Africa?

To be a solo traveller in West Africa one needs to be an experienced traveller. This is not the place to cut your teeth. As a simple example those tourists who chose to travel in the region with tour companies are

totally unaware of how challenging travel for the solo traveller moving as the locals do really is. A good example is travelling by Sept- Place car, I moved from Labe to Conakry in Guinea, a total of 190 miles in 14 hours. This was the norm. On the other hand, choosing to do as I pleased, I spent time in the Sahara Desert in Mauritania and visited the Holy City of Chingetti. I choose to go to the Highlands in Guinae and spent four days on the back of a motor bike while viewing beautiful waterfalls. Travelling this way my meals were their meals. I ate as they ate and where they ate.

I have never been able to pickup languages so I had to know how to communicate by other means in the many areas where little English was spoken. In Cameroon I got to spend half a day in a pygmy village which was extremely interesting especially now that there are only a small number of pygmy villages in all of Africa.

Your books seem to emphasize the cultural richness and diversity of Africa beyond stereotypes. What message do you hope readers take away from your travelogues, particularly about the countries you've explored?

My hope is that my writing can play a role in myth busting. I am yet to see a woman in a grass skirt. I hope that the term "poor" can be put into a better, more accurate perspective. In most villages no one earns $1,000 per month but most live a good balanced life where family values still matter and crime is still low. One change I would like to see is for NGOs to take the native people into the most senior decision-making roles. This will help to ensure NGO money is put to the best use.

I have seen many small children in the streets during school time. I learnt that, although school was free, these children had neither uniforms nor books. Here the NGOs, at a very small cost, could put a program in place to have a unform exchange so that children who could not afford could be given uniforms. Simple but potentially very powerful.

How has your background in accounting and government influenced your approach to

writing and documenting your travel experiences? What advice would you give to aspiring travelers who want to explore regions like West Africa independently but may feel apprehensive about safety or logistics?**

Because of my accounting background I can quickly convert when someone is trying to sell me something. So it's not too often that I have been ripped off. In fact, it is quite the opposite as the price demanded many times is so much less than I expect to pay. I do not barter very hard because I always consider the other party has a family at home so if the price is a good price for me the bartering ends.

Having had a long government career, I see problems and am upset when there is no action taken on those problems that can be quickly resolved.

In one country people travelling from city to city must show their ID but many times this has been damaged and so much hassle ensues at the stop points including on the spot fines. Sometimes the holder of the ID has been trying to have it replaced for one or more years. To me this is unacceptable.

I would encourage experienced, confident travellers to go solo in West Africa but this is not the place for the inexperienced. Thanks to sound research, I did not feel safety was an issue but logistics can be a nightmare if you do not know how to deal with them.

PHOTO: Sarah Albee, bestselling author, brings history and science to life through captivating storytelling in children's literature.

Unveiling the Curious Mind

SARAH ALBEE

Exploring the Intersection of History, Science, and Creativity in Children's Literature

Sarah Albee, bestselling author, discusses her eclectic journey and creative process, blending history with engaging storytelling to inspire young minds.

Sarah Albee is the New York Times bestselling author of over 150 captivating books for children, spanning from preschool to middle grade. Her recent nonfiction works have garnered accolades such as Junior Library Guild, Bank Street College of Education Best Books, and Notable Social Studies Trade Books selections, along with winning the esteemed Eureka! Nonfiction Children's Book Awards. With a penchant for intertwining history and science, Albee crafts educational experiences that spark curiosity and engage young minds.

Before delving into the world of full-time writing, Albee embarked on diverse adventures that shaped her unique perspective. From shooting hoops on college courts to playing semi-professional basketball in Cairo, Egypt, her experiences cultivated a rich tapestry of insights and inspirations. Notably, her nine-year tenure at Children's Television Workshop, the powerhouse behind Sesame Street, honed her ability to think like a child and infuse her writing with humor, resonating deeply with young readers.

Albee's creative process is a testament to her boundless curiosity and analytical mind. From her book *"Fairy Tale Science,"* where she melds beloved tales with scientific inquiry, to her unconventional explorations of history in works like *"Bugged: How Insects Changed History"* and *"Poop Happened: A History of the World from the Bottom Up,"* she consistently unveils the lesser-known facets of the past. Through accessible storytelling and hands-on experiments, she transforms seemingly mundane topics into captivating narratives that captivate and educate young readers.

Her forthcoming projects promise to captivate audiences anew. With upcoming releases such as *"The Painter and the President: Gilbert Stuart's Brush with George Washington"* and *"Bounce! A Scientific History of Rubber,"* illustrated by acclaimed artists Stacy Innerst and Eileen Ryan Ewen respectively, Albee continues to push the boundaries of children's literature.

Intrigued by topics that pique her interest, whether it's the evolution of sanitation or the challenges faced by historical women navigating societal norms, Albee's writing transcends conventional boundaries. With each book, she endeavors to instill a sense of wonder

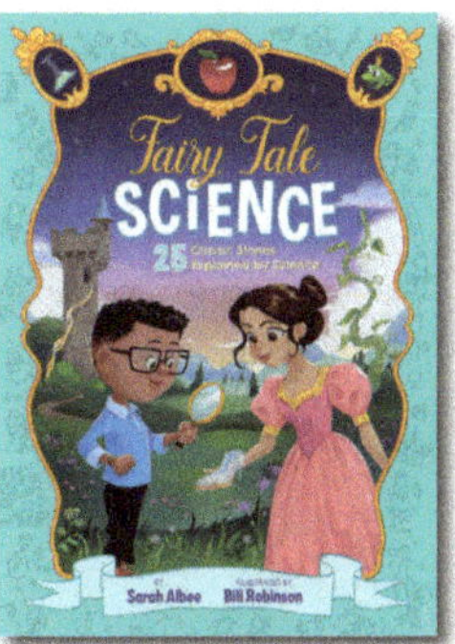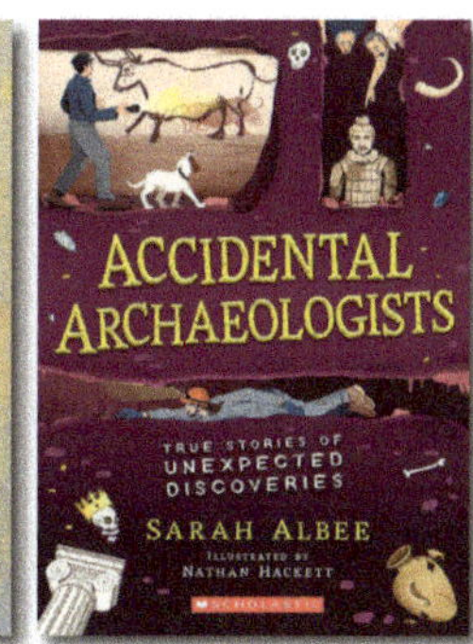

Dive into a world of wonder with Sarah Albee's latest book, blending history and science in an engaging narrative for young readers.

and curiosity in her readers, guiding them on a journey through the fascinating intersection of history and science.

How did your diverse experiences, from playing basketball in Egypt to working at Sesame Workshop, influence your journey towards becoming a prolific children's nonfiction author?

I'm never sure if I can draw a direct causal link between a life experience and a cool book idea, but I do think it's been helpful to have had lots of different jobs and to have lived in many different places. I learned Arabic while playing on a basketball team with a fantastic group of Egyptian women, and I also pursued my lifelong interest in archaeology while there. (I'd also taken a year off from college to work at an archaeology institute in Italy.) That's probably a good origin story for my book Accidental Archaeologists. And my nine years at Sesame Street trained me to think like a kid, write for kids, and, happily, to appreciate that I can write with humor, because kids love to laugh just as much as adults do.

Your books often blend history with engaging storytelling and hands-on experiments, such as in "Fairy Tale Science." Can you share insights into your creative process for developing these unique educational experiences?

I absolutely loved fairy tales as a kid, but I always had a rather—cough!—analytical mind, and was constantly interrupting my parent or babysitter with questions: "Could a pair of glass slippers survive an evening of ballroom dancing?" or "What kind of poison was in the apple that Snow White ate?" or "Could Rapunzel's hair support the weight of a prince?" Whether or not they found such questions charming, they did not adequately answer them, so I filed these questions into my brain database and then explored them as an adult. So Fairy Tale Science was a natural consequence—I have a synopsis of each fairy tale, and then ask one or more scientific questions about it, and then kids can do experiments to test it out.

From Bugged: How Insects Changed History to Poop Happened: A History of the World from the Bottom Up, to Troublemakers in Trousers: Women and What They Wore to Get Things Done, your book topics are both fascinating and unconventional. What draws you to explore these lesser-known aspects of history, and how do you make them accessible and entertaining for young readers?

I write about things that fascinate me, and hope I can show kids that history does not need to be all about battles and dates and royal successions (well, unless there's a cool poisoning story behind the royal succession). I'm much more interested in social history—what ordinary people ate, or wore, or did for a living; what happened when they got sick, or how they relieved themselves before toilets were invented.

My Bugged book was something of a follow-up to my Poop book, because while working on the latter, I learned that so many diseases were the result of insect-vectored pathogens.

A few years ago I wrote a book for National Geographic called Why'd They Wear That? and in researching that book I became fascinated by the challenges so many women faced for most of history, negotiating the world in long skirts. And later, I began collecting stories of women from history who flouted convention/the law and dressed in men's clothing, at times when that ranged from highly improper to an executable offense. They dressed that way for a range of reasons—to fight for their country, escape enslavement, rule, become a pirate, etc. That book, Troublemakers in Trousers came out in 2022. It gave me the chance to write about a lot of women I've long admired.

Basically, I try to find a topic kids are interested in—poop, bugs, clothing, dogs, poison—and then I trace it chronologically through history.

What genres do you typically write in?

Pre-pandemic, most of my books were long-form middle grade nonfiction, with historical images. But I believe that kids lost a lot of ground during the pandemic, and that they need more visual support when reading. So my next four books are going to be nonfiction picture books, for a slightly older reader (7 – 10 or so). Picture books are SO challenging to write, but I love the process.

Can you provide some information about your most popular or award-winning books?

Perhaps my best-selling book is Accidental Archaeologists: True Stories of Unexpected Discoveries. It's about ordinary people—farmers, construction workers, hikers, kids—who accidentally stumbled across major archaeological discoveries that changed what we thought we knew about history.

But perhaps the book that will be on my tombstone is Poop Happened: A History of the World from the Bottom Up. It's several years old, but still a very popular title. It's about the history of sanitation, which is arguably the history of human civilization, because societies that paid attention to how to get rid of waste tended to survive and thrive.

Are there any upcoming releases or projects that you're working on?

I have two new books coming out this summer/fall! In August, I have a picture book called The Painter and the President: Gilbert Stuart's Brush with George Washington. Gilbert Stuart was the go-to portrait painter of the late 1700s/early 1800s, and he painted George three times. All three paintings have become iconic, but the fun part is, they couldn't stand one another! It's illustrated by the incredible Stacy Innerst.

And in October, I have a book called Bounce! A Scientific History of Rubber. That one's illustrated by Eileen Ryan Ewen.

Len Handeland discusses his transition from fashion to writing, his fascination with the supernatural, and how his diverse experiences influence his captivating vampire and paranormal novels.

Len Handeland, acclaimed author of supernatural and crime drama novels, shares insights into his creative journey and storytelling inspirations.

Master of the Supernatural

LEN HANDELAND

HOW DIVERSE EXPERIENCES SHAPE HIS PARANORMAL NARRATIVES

AS TOLD TO BEN ALAN

Len Handeland is a multifaceted storyteller whose journey from the world of fashion and beauty to the realm of writing has been nothing short of extraordinary. Known for his captivating vampire, paranormal, and murder crime drama novels, Len has carved a niche for himself in the literary world. His debut novel, *The Darkest Gift*, not only garnered critical acclaim but also caught the attention of major networks for potential adaptation into a mini-series or motion picture. With a repertoire that includes titles like *Requiem for Miriam, Tales from the Chair, Transplanted Evil*, and *The Darkest Passages*, Len continues to enthrall readers with his imaginative narratives. As he prepares to release his sixth novel, "The Haunting of Wellsley Manor," in the fall of 2024, Len shares insights into how his diverse career experiences have shaped his storytelling. From the creative flair of fashion illustration to the allure of modeling and the aesthetic sensibilities of hairstyling, each profession has left an indelible mark on his writing. In this interview, Len delves into the themes that inspire his work, the unique blend of genres he explores, and the emotional depth he brings to his characters, offering readers a glimpse into the mind of a writer who seamlessly weaves the supernatural with the human experience.

Your career journey spans from fashion illustration and modeling to hair styling and now writing. How have these diverse experiences influenced your storytelling, and do you find elements of these professions reflected in your books?

Each of my past professions helped to influence my writing. My experience in fashion illustration, where I used creativity and imagination to design, was also applied to writing. I also learned to apply what I learned in modeling to my writing when I was told by many photographers to "make love to the camera" so the look was sultry and alluring. Each of the three vampire characters seduces others with their looks; they are devastatingly handsome, sultry, and dangerously deadly. In hairstyling, the business of aesthetics deals with the principles of beauty and artistic taste; each vampire took exceptional pride in their appearance, and each character's devastatingly good looks were used to seduce their victims.∑

Your first novel, The Darkest Gift, delves into themes of love, jealousy, and the supernatural. What inspired you to explore these themes through the lens of vampirism and paranormal experiences, and how do you balance horror with the emotional depth of your characters?

I chose to explore the subject of vampirism due to my lifelong fascination with vampires and their immortal existence. Love is infinite. Some argue that emotions such as jealousy and hatred can also feel as eternal as love. In my book, the horror aspect is essential to each vampire character, while the emotional depth of each character is balanced with it. Two of the characters are reluctant vampires, striving to hold on to human emotions such as love and tenderness and longing for companionship. On the contrary, the other vampire is consumed by rage, jealousy, and a thirst for power, blood, and revenge.

In Requiem for Miriam, you introduce a blend of murder, crime drama, and the paranormal. What drew you to merge these genres, and how do you approach building suspense and maintaining the reader's engagement throughout the narrative?

In a typical murder crime drama novel, the victim's life ends once the crime has been committed. I wanted to create a unique story where the perpetrator of the crime feels the victim's presence, and the detectives are solving it, essentially assisting them. At the same time, the entity seeks justice from beyond the grave. I kept the readers' interest

in the narrative by exploring each character's background. Like viewers, readers long for an emotional connection with a character. If a character has depth and their background is known to the reader/viewer, it keeps them engaged throughout the story.

Your book Tales from the Chair offers a behind-the-scenes look at your life in the hair industry. How did writing about your personal and professional experiences differ from crafting fiction, and what insights do you hope readers gain from this memoir?

Reflecting on a past profession or writing a memoir is quite different from creating a work of fiction. It's about conveying real experiences, interactions, and emotions compared to pure imagination. Tales from the Chair was written to bring closure to my 27-year career in the hair industry. It also offers advice to those entering the industry and salon owners, drawing from my experiences owning three hair salons.

With your novels often featuring paranormal and supernatural elements, how do you conduct research to create believable and immersive worlds, and what sources of inspiration do you draw upon for these fantastical aspects?

I have been a devoted horror fan throughout my life, having read numerous novels by well-known authors such as Stephen King, Clive Barker, Dean Koontz, and the late Anne Rice. All of these writers have influenced my writing style. Additionally, I grew up watching many horror movies and television shows that dealt with the supernatural, which also heavily influenced my writing. As far as research goes: I have witnessed paranormal activity and seen videos of people claiming that entities haunted their homes. Overall, I have a deep interest in parapsychology.

Your upcoming novel, The Darkest Passages, is a sequel to The Darkest Gift. How did you approach continuing the story and developing your characters further, and what new themes or challenges can readers expect in this sequel?

As a writer, I need to be emotionally invested in my story and characters, just like the readers. "The Darkest Gift" is my first novel and holds a special place in my heart. Although I hadn't initially planned for a sequel, I received messages from readers asking if there would be one. After careful thought, I continued the story, introducing new themes and challenges. In the sequel, one of the vampires encounters vampire royalty in a different location and learns about others who share a similar desire for revenge against another vampire, Stefan. The sequel introduces new characters, including a renowned vampire hunter who becomes an unlikely ally. An entire chapter is dedicated to the history of the feared and loathed vampire Stefan, with a shocking secret revealed. Together, they unite to seek revenge against Stefan.

Thomas J. Yeggy, esteemed author and legal expert, shares his profound insights into human behavior and global affairs.

Exploring the Human Psyche

THOMAS J. YEGGY
A LEGAL MIND ON GLOBAL AFFAIRS

AS TOLD TO Z. ROBERTS

Thomas J. Yeggy is a man of many dimensions, whose career and life experiences have shaped a unique perspective on the human condition and global affairs. A University of Iowa Law graduate, Yeggy has spent decades practicing law in Davenport, Iowa, and Rock Island, Illinois, and serving as a mental health judge. His tenure of over 25 years in the judiciary has provided him with profound insights into the complexities of human behavior, insights that permeate his writing. With more than 1,500 authored opinions and minimal reversals, Yeggy's legal acumen is well-established.

Beyond the courtroom, Yeggy's interests extend into the realm of global security, particularly the control of nuclear weapons. His fascination with this subject was ignited by the historical events of Hiroshima and Nagasaki and further fueled by Robert McNamara's reflections on the Cuban Missile Crisis. This interest culminated in his First Strike series, where he explores the precarious balance of power during the Cold War. Yeggy's work is a blend of meticulous research and creative storytelling, weaving historical accuracy with fictional narratives to engage readers in thought-provoking ways.

Currently residing in Pensacola Beach, Florida, Yeggy enjoys the tranquility of the Gulf of Mexico, which serves as a backdrop for his writing endeavors. Summers are spent in Davenport, where he cherishes time with his grandchildren, Jeff and Ashley Brown, and their beloved dogs, Otis and Emme. Through his writing, Yeggy invites readers to ponder the delicate interplay between law, human nature, and the geopolitical tensions that have shaped our world.

With your extensive background in law and psychology, as well as your long tenure as a judge handling mental health and substance abuse cases,

"Mushroom Cloud" is a riveting blend of history and fiction, offering a thought-provoking exploration of Cold War tensions and human resilience.

how have your professional experiences influenced your writing, particularly your insights into human nature and conflict?

I often found myself asking why a human behaves as they do in many situations and developed my theories based on psychological concepts.

I became a Neo- Freudian in the Erik Erikson epigenetics sense; in that I believe that the personality is developed over several stages. But I am Freudian in firmly believing that the id must be kept in check by criminal laws that are enforced by forces like Hobbes Leviathan.

The short history of the US has seen the Country go from a time when there was authoritarian rule, evidencing a need for individual rights to be developed, to present day where the sovereign has sur-

Thomas J. Yeggy masterfully combines legal expertise and historical insight, crafting compelling narratives that challenge readers to rethink global conflicts.

rendered to the "smash and grab" mentality driven by the id. So, my writing finds that the sovereign must control the id in all of us to have civilization survive.

Your fascination with the development and control of nuclear weapons is evident in your First Strike series. What sparked your initial interest in this subject, and how did it evolve over the years to inspire you to write these books?

Vasily Arkhipov and the courage he demonstrated on the 27th day of October 1962 while aboard the Soviet submarine B-59 where he refused to allow Captain Savitsky to fire a nuclear tipped torpedo at the aircraft carrier USS

Essex, thereby preventing WW III.

The second issue that caught my attention was why the US did not make a preventative counter-force strike against the Soviets sometime between October of 1961 and December of 1963 when they had the chance to rid the world of the Soviets weapons that they had used essentially enslaving 200 million people for 45 years behind the Iron Curtain.

In Mushroom Cloud, you introduce Dr. Caleb Young, a character deeply embedded inhistorical events. How did you balance historical accuracy with fictional elements in crafting his story, and what research was involved in creating this character and his world?

I was particularly interested in the scientists that guided the free world in their fight against the Axis and later the Soviet Union. Caleb became a composite of those men and women. He becomes a pacifist like many of the scientist, but begrudgingly realized that the monsters hiding beneath our beds are there and must be dealt with by humans that can stomach some blood.

Your First Strike series delves into significant historical confrontations between the United States and the Soviet Union during the Cold War. How do you approach weaving real historical events into your narrative, and what challenges do you face in maintaining authenticity while keeping the story engaging?

I researched. The research was painstakingly lengthy but enjoyable. For example, I had occasion to contact the author of Black Tuesday over Namsai. Colonel Earl McGill. He flew B-29s in Korea. He is 95 but gave me great advice and a keen insight into that era. I went through over 10,000

pages of textbooks, novels and articles over five years searching for interesting side stories.

As for history I have my reservations. Even mainstream history is not linear in the sense that one set of circumstances dictates a certain result to come repeatedly. The only constant in my lifetime has been US engagement in useless wars.

History must be revised to consider facts previously undiscovered and perhaps that is how results vary. I've taken many facts and made reasonable

deductions and conclusions from them to create a history that fits my narrative. For example, history does not record the fact that the US CIA had an op that was designed to deceive the Soviets about the capabilities of the B-36 but based on logical deductions I have concluded that they did and created 'Operation Anaconda" to chronicle that conclusion.

Keep in mind that my history is not contradicted by the facts but is complementary to them. For example, in Mushroom Cloud I have created two other CIA operations that based upon any reasonable reading of the tea

leaves had to have taken place but there is no record of them in recorded history.

Given your extensive legal background, what parallels do you draw between legal conflicts and the geopolitical tensions explored in your books? How do these parallels enhance your storytelling?

I must cede many of my individual rights to the Sovereign to have an orderly society and not the other way around. Similarly, you must be able to defend yourself from the Id persona of

a hostile nation because many nations do not have a conscience –superego. They will feed their hedonistic desires with your assets unless you have at least minimal deterrence. I end Book III by resorting to society being regulated by Platonic principles found in Book VIII of the Republic. The most important point is that the Philosopher King Ruling Class cannot own property. The politicians in almost every nation fall prey to the temptation to exert their power to exploit the masses for their personal economic gain.

You have spent summers in Davenport and currently reside in Pensacola Beach, Florida. How do these locations influence your writing environment, and do they contribute to your creative process in any specific ways?

The Gulf of Mexico is beautiful and inspiring. Most of my writing is done in our Condo at the Portofino overlooking the beach I have a huge world map on the wall in front of my desk and marvel at the fact that we have not blown ourselves up given that we have had so many close calls. I need to close with saying that I wish humans were less hegemonic and more altruistic but for many thousands of years we have had constant wars.

Exploring History and Mystery with
JULIE ANDERSON

Unearthing Secrets in Post-War London

Julie Anderson discusses her latest historical novel "The Midnight Man," set in 1940s London, highlighting post-war societal changes and female empowerment.

BY ANNA HARLOWE

Julie Anderson, the CWA Dagger-listed author of the acclaimed Whitehall thrillers and historical adventure stories for young adults, has a knack for weaving intricate tales of intrigue and suspense. Her journey from a senior civil servant to a celebrated crime fiction writer is as fascinating as her novels. In this exclusive interview for Reader's House Magazine, Julie Anderson discusses her latest novel, "The Midnight Man," set in post-war London, and her return to the genre she adores: historical fiction.

Revisiting Post-War London: The Inspiration Behind The Midnight Man

Set in the 1940s, *The Midnight Man* is the first book in Anderson's Clapham Trilogy. She shares, "I wanted my next book to have contemporary relevance, especially after the pandemic, but I didn't want to write about COVID. So I decided to write about a similar time when, after a great and tragic global upheaval, people were adjusting to a new reality. The obvious parallel was the period after World War II. An outpouring of relief and joy that it was over was followed by austerity and

hard times. Some people wanted to return to how things were before, others had ideas about how things should change. The difference being that in the UK from 1945 onwards a new society was being forged. I suppose I also wanted to remind people of what was possible."

Anderson's choice of Clapham as the setting was deeply personal. Having lived there for over thirty years, she was intrigued by the South London Hospital for Women & Children. "When I began researching, I discovered that it was the largest woman-only hospital in the UK, run exclusively by and for women. This made it both unusual and very apposite for my book," she explains. The post-war era, with its complex dynamics of gender roles and societal expectations, provided a rich backdrop for exploring themes of female enfranchisement and professional ambition against remnants of wartime camaraderie and struggle.

From Whitehall to Clapham: A Shift in Genre

Transitioning from contemporary Whitehall thrillers to historical fiction, Anderson finds herself returning to familiar yet uncharted

waters. "The Midnight Man is a return to writing in a genre I love," she says. Anderson's previous experience with historical settings, such as her young adult series set in 13th century Al Andalus, equipped her well for the challenge. However, she notes that capturing 1940s London was markedly different. "Much of everyday life then was the same or similar to now, like having household electricity, piped running water, cars and buses, none of which was available in thirteenth century Spain," she points out.

Her Whitehall thrillers, including the CWA Dagger-listed "Opera," were grounded in her extensive knowledge of the inner workings of the British government. "The machinations of ambitious politicians and top officials provide plenty of scope for intrigue and, in 'Opera,' espionage," she reflects. Yet, the historical mysteries offer a different kind of storytelling challenge and reward, requiring meticulous research and a keen sense of period detail to bring past eras vividly to life.

A New Series with Contemporary Resonance

Anderson's passion for history and storytelling shines through in

"The Midnight Man." By delving into the lives of women at the South London Hospital for Women & Children, she not only crafts a compelling murder mystery but also highlights the resilience and determination of women in the face of societal change. "The South London had to constantly prove its worth and credentials, often against opposition from the predominantly male establishment. As did the women who worked there," she says, underscoring the novel's themes of perseverance and progress.

In "The Midnight Man," readers will find a rich tapestry of historical intrigue, gender politics, and personal triumphs, all set against the vivid backdrop of post-war London. For fans of Julie Anderson's work, this new series promises to be as enthralling and thought-provoking as her previous novels, offering a perfect blend of historical authenticity and gripping storytelling.

As Anderson embarks on this new literary journey, she invites readers to explore the untold stories of the past, reminding us all of the enduring power of hope, change, and the human spirit.

Mastering the Art of Storytelling and Portraiture
TERRENCE A. REESE
A Conversation with the Best-Selling Author and Photographer

Terrence A. Reese captivates with his profound storytelling, enriching readers' lives through his insightful and educational literary and artistic works.

Terrence A. Reese, a name synonymous with evocative portraiture and impactful storytelling, stands as a luminary in the literary and artistic realms. Best known for his seminal work "Reflections," Reese has etched his place in history with what he aptly describes as "the Best Coffee Table Book of Portraiture of Iconic African Americans ever created." His journey as a writer, intriguingly sparked at his grandfather's funeral when he was just ten years old, showcases the profound intersections of personal experiences and creative expression. Reese's oeuvre is marked by an unyielding commitment to education through art, a testament to his belief that literature's greatest power lies in its ability to impart life lessons. This philosophy resonates deeply in his latest works, where he deftly explores the nuances of human relationships and the vital importance of intimacy and financial acumen—subjects he passionately argues are grossly neglected in today's education system.

In a captivating interview with Reader's House Magazine, Reese opens up about his inspirations, his admiration for literary giants like Toni Morrison and James Baldwin, and his thoughts on the transformative power of storytelling. He also shares insights into his latest project, "The Science of Seduction: The Descendants," a sequel poised to delve into the complexities of love and progress across generations.

Reese's reflections offer not just a glimpse into his creative mind but also a profound commentary on the societal values he holds dear. His advocacy for truth, honesty, and practical knowledge as cornerstones of a well-rounded education speaks volumes about his mission to enlighten and inspire through his multifaceted body of work. As readers navigate his insightful narratives, they are invited to join Reese in a dialogue that challenges, educates, and ultimately enriches their understanding of the world.

When did you start writing?

The day of my grandfather's funeral. I was ten years old.

My shiny shoes stood behind the line in front of my grandfather's home. I'm clean as a whistle wearing one of the two suits I have. All eyes are on me as I bent my knees, swung my arm back and then moved it forward slowly.

The penny flew from between my fingers. Everyone standing on both sides of the sidewalk watched the penny fly through the air, bounce on the sidewalk and into the line.

I cheered and high five everyone around me.

How did you get to this point in your life as a writer?

"Reflections made me a Best-Selling Author, because it's the Best Coffee Table Book of Portraiture of Iconic African Americans ever created. There may be other books, but the concept of Reflections is a work of Art that Educates. No one can dispute that!"

If you could meet any writer, dead or alive, who would it be?

Toni Morrison, James Baldwin, Billy Wilder, Orson Wells, Ian Fleming, William Wyler, Stephen King, Mario Puzo. And what would you want to know? Nothing. Their opportunities wouldn't have been mine. I would like to have lunch with them and talk about ideas and concepts.

What moves you most in a work of literature?

The ability to teach a person something that will be useful in their lives.

What books and authors have impacted your writing career?

Orson Wells (Citizen Kane), Ian Fleming (007), Mario Puzo (The Godfather)

Which writers — working today do you admire?

J. K. Rowling. I just read the Harry Potter series.

What made you write The Science of Seduction?

To help people understand the importance of intimacy in a romantic relationship. When a person thinks, 'I wish I would have known then what I do now.' That's a painful revelation. If a person isn't taught, they can only fake it for so long until it's revealed. Being an attentive, good lover is something that's taught. It doesn't just happen.

In The Science of Seduction Lena writes the Black Book, which teaches a boy how to cater to the Needs, Wants and Desires of a Woman. It also suggests things a woman can do to keep a man interested. It's a give and take. A two-way street that has to be respected.

Lena is a product of her environment. At 18 she carries the knowledge of a woman twice her age, because her parents have pulled the curtains of reality away and allowed her to see the world for what it is.

What are you working on?

The Science of Seduction: The Descendants. How does the next generation handle the problems that arise because of progress? Is Love a Sacrifice or a Motivation?

What do you think should be improved in the education of our children?

The two most important things in society aren't taught: Intimacy and How to please your partner. How to manage your finances. Parents send their children into the world on hopes and prayers. Then the consequences of their lack of communication walks through the front door. And then they are speechless. What do we lack as a people? Truth and Honesty.

What would you say to your readers?

Enjoy yourself.

Available in
PRINT

Americas to Australia Europe to Africa Reader's House is available over 190 countries and thousands of retaiers, platforms including Amazon, Barnes & Noble, Walmart, Waterstone's .....

ELECTRONIC

It is an electronic (flip book) format and interactive. Accessable from electronic devices like pc, smart phone, notepads..

ONLINE

All interviews, we conduct make them accessable online for free.

SOCIAL MEDIA

We are on Facebook, Instagram and X. Please follow us on social media @readershousemag

contact us today for an interview opportunity at
editor@readershouse.co.uk

<table>
<tr><td rowspan="20">Subscribe Now!</td></tr>
</table>

YES! I would like a subscription to

☐ Current Issue for   ☐ Includes Shipping and Handling

☐ One-Year Subscription (_______ Issues) for

☐ Two-Year Subscription (_______ Issues) for

☐ I am a renewing a current subscription   ☐ I am a new subscriber

Name: _______________________________   Phone: _______________

Shipping Address: _______________________________

Billing Address: _______________________________

Email: _______________________________

☐ Yes, I would like to receive updates, newsletters and special offers
☐ No, I would NOT like to receive updates, newsletters and special offers

Payment Type: ☐ Cash   ☐ Check

Please mail this form to:
Magazine Name: *Reader's House* by Newyox 200 Suite, 134-146 Curtain Road EC2A 3AR London   readershouse.co.uk